BEHIND
PICKETWIRE

BEHIND PICKETWIRE

—

M. DAY HAMPTON

Copyright © 2020 HuckleberryBlue Press

Published by HuckleberryBlue Press, Paradise, CA
MDayHampton.com

Edited and designed by Girl Friday Productions
www.girlfridayproductions.com

Cover design: Emily Weigel
Project management: Bethany Davis

Image credits: cover © Shutterstock/frankie's, Shutterstock/Julia Tochilina, Shutterstock/Here, Shutterstock/Ksenia Merenkova, Shutterstock/one AND only

ISBN (paperback): 978-1-7346966-0-8
ISBN (ebook): 978-1-7346966-1-5
Library of Congress Control Number: 2020917680

First edition

To Jennifer. Writing a novel is hard. Fortunately, I had no clue of this fact beforehand. Luckily, Jennifer's expectations for me were unyielding. She is my champion. She is the one who picked up my early drafts off the floor, unwrinkled them, and handed them back, the one who rescued my computer from being thrown out because of my ineptness, the one who endlessly read rewrite after rewrite, and the one who drove me across the country for research and inspiration to places God wouldn't even have gone. Her unwavering support and love along with her "let's make it happen" attitude is the only reason you have this book.

To Howard and Maurine Johnson (more on them later).

ACKNOWLEDGMENTS

A special thank you to Mary Kole at Kidlit, for your honesty, humor, and encouragement. You, my friend, are simply amazing.

To Girl Friday Productions. All of you epitomize professionalism, but more importantly, you freely and gracefully shared your personal pledge to me and my story. From Christina Henry de Tessan to manager extraordinaire Bethany Davis. Ingrid Emerick wrapped her arms around me and my manuscript and hasn't let go yet. To Michelle Hope Anderson and Clete Barrett Smith's editorial talent; Rachel Marek's stunning design mind; and Georgie Hockett along with Katie Meyers, whose marketing prowess made all things happen.

To my friends and family who shared the gift of their time so effortlessly, their heartfelt critiques, great ideas, and candor, all of which is a testament to how truly blessed I am.

For all of you, I am grateful.

CHAPTER 1

They say there's a difference between living and existing, and he'd miserably failed at both. Red Johnson fumbled with the contents of his left pants pocket: a weathered key, thirty-eight cents in assorted change, a small pocketknife, and a handful of pills prescribed for all the ailments God had cursed him with after sixty-eight years. Things that weighed him down, things he'd accumulated, the sum of life in one pocket. He rubbed the change against the plain, worn gold band on his arthritic finger.

He wanted to curse aloud. Curse about growing old, slowing down, and falling apart. He couldn't even pee with enthusiasm. Of all the items in that pocket, he only needed that wedding band he'd worn for thirty years.

He rolled the medications in his palm as Addy briskly cleared dishes from the kitchen table.

"Don't put those in your pocket. You'll forget to take them." Addy rechecked the Tupperware pill container, confirmed Tuesday's empty slot, and snapped the lid closed. "Don't forget, I'll be home late this afternoon. You and Jake will have to forage for your own lunch, but tonight, I'll make us a big pot of spaghetti. Take out some hamburger from the freezer, OK?"

Jake heard his name and came alert, wagging his tail.

"Jake has plenty of dog food in front of him." Red's crooked finger pointed to the floor. "Look, it's all over the floor. He needs to learn how to eat with his mouth shut. It's been eight years now." Red looked up at his wife. He cleared his throat and leaned back into the kitchen chair. "Why don't you just stay home today, Addy?"

She took a quick breath, smiled, and kissed him on the cheek. "I've already told you. Today is doctor day for my brother, he's waiting for me. Then I've got to stop at the office and help Matthew with some escrow papers." She gathered her briefcase, sweater, and reading glasses. "Why don't you go outside today, rake up the leaves and pine needles?"

Red curled up his lips and shook his head. "Yard man comin' tomorrow." Why exert energy today when it will be accomplished by someone else, tomorrow?

"Red, you need to go outside. Enjoy the fresh air. Get the stink off! And be productive."

"It's cold outside." Red crossed his arms.

"Put your coat on." Addy opened the kitchen door, paused, picked up a notepad from the counter, and held it up toward Red. "Here's the grocery list. Try to stick to it this time, OK."

"I'm probably not gonna have time today, honey."

Addy stared at Red, her head slightly tilted forward.

He wasn't quite sure if he had been convincing enough. "I got a lot going on today."

He waited for the eye roll. Red knew she loved him, cherished him, all faults and attitude included. Perhaps it was healthier—no, easier—for her to let things go rather than stir long-buried emotions. She tightened her lips. If she had words, they remained inside.

"Why don't you just stop at the market on your way home from work?"

There it was. He knew it, the final insufferable morning act that would frustrate her into slamming the door, but not before saying her piece. "I'll take 'How to Piss Off Your Wife' for five hundred, Alex."

Red grunted, wrinkled his lips, and then noticed Jake's stare. "What are you lookin' at?" Red waited until Addy's car left the driveway. Now was his opportunity to flush the godforsaken drugs that threatened to preserve his aging innards while his muscles, bones, and spirit deteriorated with each passing year.

After thirty years of marriage, he expected his life to end peacefully with his wife. Red wanted to die in her arms, and that was all right in his eyes. Addy showed no expectation of slowing down in the near future and planned on taking Red along for the ride. And that was all right in her eyes.

Two short bursts of a car horn brought his gaze up to the window. He could barely see the white Jeep approaching the group of mailboxes at the end of the drive. Charlotte had been the rural mail carrier for years and always gave a honk when delivering the mail. Red liked Charlotte and enjoyed their brief conversations on mindless matters, and on most occasions, she purposely, but briefly, paused her appointed rounds for the banter.

By the time Red walked down the long driveway, the Jeep was gone. His mailbox was the first of about eight or nine of different colors, heights, and conditions, all precariously attached to a long, unsteady two-by-six board perched upon two questionable posts. One box had a purple heart painted on its side above the owner's name, another used a frayed bungee cord to keep the door from flailing about, and one had no door at all. He leaned against the end for support but quickly realized the wobbly assemblage was worse off than him.

Red looked up into the enormous oak tree at the end of the driveway. The giant limbs seemed to moan with the wind as its leaves rustled high above. He couldn't see the top. It was the largest oak tree in the neighborhood, maybe in the county. Even the conifers concealing the two houses across the street couldn't match its breadth.

A pair of large, rusty wrought-iron gates stood open, leading up into the Johnsons' driveway. The gates were too ornate for the neighborhood, but Addy insisted they were perfect. Their patina alone proved worthy of salvage. They'd rescued them from an old barn purchased in a real estate deal. No one knew their origin, their history. Red named them Pollux and Castor after the Gemini twins constellation. The gates served no purpose. They were never closed. Addy wouldn't hear of it. Red, on the other hand, would've rather had them closed at all times. As far as he was concerned, anyone who dared to come onto the property better be in possession of a warrant or a pizza.

They'd built the house many years ago on a secluded parcel of land set well off the county road in a forest of old-growth conifers and mixed oak trees. The long driveway forced Red to take a break midway. The rain began before he was halfway back to the house. Out of breath, he placed the rummaged pile of mail on the kitchen table and wiped the rain from his face.

The storm winds made the house feel small, vulnerable. The walls creaked with each gust of wind, and windows seemed to bow inward as the rain pelted the glass. Rainwater dripped from the middle of the ceiling and ran down the light fixture hanging over the kitchen table, falling on the mail. Letters addressed to Addy, soaked.

It was an elusive roof leak, returning even after several do-it-yourself fixes. He moved the pile of mail to the kitchen counter and cursed as he stomped to the screen door. Addy's mutt lay on the back step. The lumbering retriever, weighing close to a hundred pounds, growled at the man as the large, sloppy rain boots clumsily passed over him. Red held on to the doorframe, barely keeping his balance. He gritted his teeth and looked at the dog. "Don't mind me. Just trying to get out of my own house without breaking a hip."

Jake had been a good dog but was not without issues. His smooth, thick, long coat was variegated in yellow, golden, but mostly red hair. His head was boxy, and his eyes were a piercing amber encircled with dark lashes, making it look like an artist had painted him with eyeliner. It gave him a soft look of majestic kindness, which Addy's heart was unable to resist. Jake adored Addy, always doting at her side, while saving his disdain for tall men, especially those inclined to wear hats. Red had long since relinquished any standing within the family. Jake was simply an obstacle, and an unpredictable one at that.

Red retrieved the aluminum extension ladder and shoved the feet hard into the ground. He squinted, the blowing rain hitting his face. The awkward weight of the ladder top slammed it into the satellite dish perched on the roof's edge. The dish was pushed into the weatherhead.

The sound of thunder shattered with paralyzing vibrations. An explosion of white light enveloped his body. Forces of electricity surged inward and raced within him. He clutched his chest as if to keep his heart from being pulled out of its bond with muscle and bone. Nothing could be heard over the deep, hollow, distorted wind. The white light transformed into muted colors, then into blackness. Pain. He felt incapacitating pain convulsing through every nerve in his body.

The ground beneath him was damp. He saw only darkness but could feel the cold wetness on his back. His lungs were empty and ached with great pressure. He wanted to gasp for air, just a breath, just one more little breath. *I'm cold,* he thought. *I can feel!* He heard a cough. Then another cough. *I can hear myself coughing!* He felt muscles, his body rolling to its side. His eyes opened. Blurry colors were coming back to focus.

He was alive.

The wind was gone and the air was still. The fir trees no longer rocked back and forth but stood silent. The boughs glistened with moisture in the late-evening sun. *My God, how long have I been out?*

He breathed in deeply and felt splinters of ice deep in his bones. He wearily stood to his feet. Expecting the worst, he visually inspected his torso, legs, then hands, finding no burns, open wounds, or protruding bones. His body trembled as he realized he could have been killed.

The interior of the house sat dark and silent. He tried the light switch three times before he realized the electricity was out. Same with the telephone. Stupid power went out each time the wind blew, it seemed. His wristwatch said it was 5:38. He'd been out for hours. Addy would be coming home soon. He looked out the window, expecting to see her drive up at any moment.

Jake was gone. The damned dog was probably annoyed about missing dinner and was out pouting somewhere on the property. Or more likely, he was walking down the middle of Coutolenc Road, annoying passing neighbors, one of his favorite pastimes. He was a strange dog, rescued by Addy years ago. Addy always said he should've been a cat.

For a long time, Red had been irritated with his friends. He thought they were being overly polite and flirtatious by removing their hats every time they greeted Addy or came indoors. "You make me look bad," he would tell them later. In reality, they just didn't want to get bit.

The room was dark except for the flickering light from the wood-stove. Red abruptly stopped. He spun around and stared intently at the flames. He hadn't stoked the fire, yet it was roaring hot, just as he'd left it. "What the hell?" Had someone been there and not noticed he was passed out in the yard?

Red instantly turned toward the hallway and called out, "Addy?" He went into each room and quickly checked. "Addy? Are you in here? I got knocked off the ladder." He hurried out the back door. "Addy? Jake? Here, Jake!" Addy's car was gone. *She still must be over at her brother's.*

The yard and driveway were barely visible through the darkness. He was concerned about the dog but more anxious about how his wife would react to Jake being gone. He walked down the driveway hoping to find the dog sitting near the mailboxes. "Jake! Here, Jake!" Nothing. He whistled and kissed aloud but was only greeted with silence. His insides quivered. His near-frantic eyes surveyed back and forth. *I need the phone to call Matt. We need to find Jake before Addy gets home. She'll be devastated.* "Goddamn it, Jake, get over here!"

Nothing but stillness. An invisible, wicked stillness.

At the bottom of the driveway, the giant oak tree marked the end of the property as the gravel drive converged with the paved roadway. But the street was gone. There was an unfamiliar forest of trees before him. Red stood stiff, not believing what he was seeing, or rather, what he wasn't seeing. He felt his insides constrict. He'd felt this way before. Next would be tunnel vision and desperate thoughts. His mind tried to make logical sense of it as he ran back to the house as fast as a sixty-eight-year-old man could. Out of breath, he grabbed a flashlight. *A shotgun. Get the shotgun.* He looked at the gun's receiver, slightly opening it. His fingers fumbled with nervousness. *Yes, it's loaded. And the safety. Take off the safety.*

The flashlight beam bounced down the driveway, back and forth, back and forth. Under the giant oak, Red stood motionless. Just beyond, a forest of timber reared in a quiet mass. The feeble beam vanished into the colossal forest. The large, moss-covered oak tree at the end of the drive now looked small next to the daunting woodland. Red repeatedly looked north and south, as if he were searching up and down the street. He strained forward. There were no houses, no mailboxes, not even an electrical power line. Panic sat in his stomach, growing deeper and stronger, metastasizing until it sucked his breath away. Bursts of conflicting thoughts twisted into a whirlwind. He wanted to run, but his brain was screaming for him to hide. A gust of wind slapped his face, breathing life back into his lungs. He ran up the driveway, stumbling and gasping for air. He did not stop until he'd slammed the door behind him. His legs would no longer hold his weight. He leaned his back against the locked door and dropped to the floor.

Red shivered. He tightly folded his arms in front of his chest, warming his hands in his armpits. He stayed sitting with his knees to his chest, the shotgun on the floor next to him. As the fire died, darkness stole through the house, taking with it the last bit of false security. His muscles cramped, and he was unable to move. Never had he experienced such infinite blackness. He felt himself blink. He still had eyes. It meant he could move. But movement made noise, and noise would give his position away. He was damp and cold, and morning was far off. If he could get to his knees, he could get the blanket on the couch.

He couldn't stand up, his legs ached with stiffness. He crawled to the living room, retrieved the crocheted throw, and returned to his post. Outside, the wind blew off and on. The house moaned and creaked. A few times throughout the night, he was sure he heard a car come up the drive. Each time, he looked out the window or opened the door, only to find it was nothing but a change in the wind. He slept sporadically. It seemed daylight would never come. If it did, though, Red wasn't sure what he would find.

CHAPTER 2

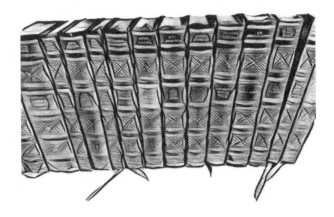

Sunlight began to enter the room. Red woke up with his shotgun across his chest. For a moment, he was disoriented. His head was spinning, his body ached. He yelled for Addy as he struggled to his feet. "Addy!" He didn't think of breakfast or coffee or even brushing his teeth. He tried the lights and phone several times before walking outside. "Addy!" He started down the driveway. "Please, God, let me be a delusional old fool." Two more steps. "I'll even take being in a bad dream." Still, no paved street, no utility lines or mailboxes. Evidence of human existence ended at the Johnson property line.

He hurried back to the house, his mind running in tight little circles. Where was Addy? What happened? Where was everyone? What about his kids, Matthew and Samantha? His grandkids? What'd happened to Jake? *Oh my God, now I know I'm crazy—I want Jake back.*

He rubbed his face with unsteady hands and tried to force rational thoughts back into his mind. He looked at himself in the mirror. His face was haggard and gray. "Please, God, help me. Whatever happened, wherever I am, just give me my family back." He watched the old man's fatigued reflection and waited. "Might as well just use the dead phone." The face in the reflection suddenly changed. *The radio!*

Red ran outside to his truck and turned on the FM first, then AM. There was nothing, not even static. He leaned back in the seat and slammed the palm of his hand onto the steering wheel. "My God. What happened to the stations? Who did this to me?"

Now he was mad. The game was over. He wanted answers. And wanted them now!

His eyes scanned his surroundings. Everything looked the same: the house, the truck, the fruit trees, the backyard, the landscaping. But two hundred yards down the driveway, another world existed. A world he hadn't asked for. The engine started on the first crank. He revved the motor, put the truck in gear, and sped down the driveway. The tires slid on the gravel. The oak tree was just ahead. He wanted out of this world. It wasn't his! His mind was strong. Stronger than anything that was possessing him. He wanted to see the paved street. He stiffened his arms, pushed on the gas pedal, and turned left, like he'd always done, just about every day.

The truck crashed down into a ditch and came to rest at the base of a large fir tree. Red was thrown about the cab and landed on the passenger seat on the downhill side.

"Son of a—" He gathered his wits, opened the passenger door, and uncontrollably plunged to the ground. "Son of a bitch!" He could see radiator fluid pour out from underneath the motor. He got back in the truck and pulled himself over to the driver's side. He restarted the engine, tried to reverse several times, but the truck wouldn't budge.

The back of the truck partially stuck up in the air, blocking where Coutolenc Road should've been. He walked due east. There used to be homes in a big meadow and an old apple orchard where Coutolenc and Hupp Roads intersected. He followed the contour of the hill, trying to keep to where the road used to be.

The forest was completely different, unlike anything he remembered. It was all virgin timber. Huge trees of sugar pine, Douglas fir, incense cedar, and ponderosa pine grew with abandon with hardly any underbrush. Near the bottom of the hill, the terrain flattened out and the meadow that he remembered came into view.

It looked almost the same, but the grass was waist high. The apple trees, homes, fences, utility poles, or any other signs of mankind were gone. Wild blackberries lined the creek. A confusion of quail, fifty birds or more, flew up in unison. The immediate sound of the whorl was so close and loud, Red was momentarily stunned. Birds. Just birds. It was the first noise he had heard of any kind away from his home. No planes, no barking dogs, no cars, not anything. The flight of the waning birds made the silence even deeper. "What the hell is going on?"

Returning home, every time Red stopped, he listened. All he caught was the wind in the trees, a bird, or nothing at all. His ears frantically searched for any man-made sound but heard only the silence of a new, unfamiliar wilderness. He was strangely thankful to find his own trail through the tall grass in the middle of the meadow. He worried about becoming lost. Would he be able to find his way home? Could his house now be gone altogether?

As he passed his pickup, he wondered if he should lock it up. Then he remembered bigger issues were at hand. A black raven was overhead. His mother always called them scavengers, the intruders, the tyrants of the bird family. Their voices had no music and their actions were without kinship. The bird circled over him for several seconds. The raven landed in the top of a tall sugar pine, its eyes locked on the man entering the house. What was their purpose really? Stupid bird.

The phone was still dead. Why would it work, with no utility poles around? Hunger and thirst set in for the first time since the day before. The darkness inside the refrigerator was a reminder that everything was going to spoil. His reading glasses were on top of the carton of eggs. *How'd those get in here?* He hooked up his propane camp stove and cooked up the raw hamburger from the day before. It was going to be for spaghetti. But things changed. He placed a small helping of cooked hamburger in Jake's empty food dish. Red opened the back door. "Jake! Here, Jake." He waited and listened for the sound of big, clumsy paws prancing on the wood deck. "Jake. Please come home, Jake." Red came inside and locked the door. He looked down at the dog dish. *Maybe some bread for him, too.*

As evening fell, Red tried to pray, but none of his prayers seemed to get past the ceiling. He made up a bed on the couch, too afraid to be away from the fire. Moments of sleep were interrupted by attacks of anxiety. His clothing was damp with sweat, and he shifted the blankets on and off throughout the night. Mundane forest sounds became inexplicable. Flashes of fear tightened his muscles and mind.

The walls flickered with firelight. He was surrounded by his wife's book collection. She loved books. He hated them. After all, why keep a book after it's been read? Addy was ten years his junior, full of grace and beauty. She loved reading and could read several books a week, some at the same time. When asked, Addy could confirm what she'd read, almost verbatim, as well as the page number.

She was a romantic married to a man who'd become practical and was heading toward pessimistic. He couldn't understand why someone would hold on to useless musty old books while having personal computers with endless worldwide access at their fingertips. He recalled the arguments. He wanted to take his angry words back.

Throughout the night, he struggled with thoughts of how he might have been thrown into another time. Time travel? Time warps? The only thing he knew about time travel was from when he was a kid. His older brother had threatened to knock him into the following week. "Time portals" was their new name. But that was science fiction. What about science, though, what about Einstein's theory of relativity? He lit the camp lantern and feverishly looked throughout the bookshelves. If only he could find some type of clue or answer as to what or why this thing had happened.

He quickly inventoried shelf after shelf, book after book, in his mind. He remembered the feel of electricity going through his body, the lightning, so what about electromagnetic theories? "Electricity and magnetic forces," Red mumbled to himself. He tried to remember. For the first time, Red felt ignorant—no, rather stupid, just like the raven. He grabbed his forehead and tried to recall what little he could. "Special relativity—velocity equals distance traveled divided by time." But what the hell did that mean? He closed his eyes, clenched his fists and cursed. "You stupid fool."

He turned his head sideways to read the spines. He never realized Addy must have enjoyed Zane Grey and Louis L'Amour. She even had collections of Dickens, Twain, Steinbeck, and Hemingway. Red riffled several shelves. Then he suddenly stopped and carefully pulled down an old book from a higher shelf. H. G. Wells, *The Time Machine*. It was make-believe. He wanted something new, something solid with scientific proof, something about wormholes or black holes. He needed to know. He wanted his computer, the internet, his way. H. G. Wells was subsequently discarded onto the floor.

He crouched down in the dark corner. The room strangely reminded him of an old, dusty library belonging to a mad scientist. The lantern light was weak. It cast shadows throughout the room, making it look like Dickens himself resided there. Red fought tears and rubbed his face. He sniffed in deeply and tried not to cry. His eyes focused on a set of old books in the far lower corner of the room. He leapt to his feet and hurriedly walked to the books without shifting the focus of his stare. It was the old set of outdated encyclopedias. He recalled an argument that he and Addy had years ago.

"Addy, they're useless. We have the internet now." Red was younger then as he held one of the opened oversize books in his large hand. The pages were glossy and still sleek, but the binding was worn and hung down loosely. "Look, Addy, they even have black-and-white photographs."

Addy stood beside him. She was beautiful, too beautiful to be with Red. Her hair was dark with indications of gray, which accented her round dark-blue eyes. Her skin was flawless and firm. She softly smiled. "It doesn't matter, Red. I love them." She looked small next to him. She wouldn't budge, she stood her ground. Addy smiled as she reached up and tenderly cupped his cheek. "You're older than these books, and I'm not planning on throwing you away, either."

Red slammed the book closed and tossed it down on the leather chair. As he left the room, he mumbled, "Fine, they're just dust collectors. We need more dust around here like we need a hole in the head."

Red slid to his knees and grabbed at the books, pulling three or four out of their assigned place. Addy must've harbored the set despite the argument. What an ass he'd been. He ransacked the set, looking for anything starting with "Dimension," "Portal," "Time," "Warp," "Matrix," or other relevant text.

He read aloud with impatience, resembling a speed reader, his crooked forefinger leading, going up and down and over and across the pages. There were no commas or periods and barely any pauses. One long, rapid, monotone brief: "Vortices of energy that allow matter to travel from one point in time to another . . . by passing through the portal . . . or may appear as an ordinary doorway . . . has the capability to produce magnetism . . . and these areas of distortion . . . twelve portals well known and documented . . . devil's graveyard . . . theory of relativity proves gravity electromagnetic process that create atmospheric collisions . . . déjà vu . . . Bermuda Triangle . . . presumption of present and future occupying in the same space."

It was too much information.

Red sat in the dark corner of the room for several hours. He'd succumbed to the nonsense of trying not to cry and wept easily. No one was there to see him. He thought of Addy. He remembered what she was wearing, a sweater with a big cowl-neck draped down over her shoulders, light blue and soft. Her eyes always seemed to attract light, no matter how faint. He closed his eyes and breathed in. He thought he smelled her lavender. She walked quietly but with purpose. He could always recognize the sound of her steps. He desperately wanted to hear them again.

Red was a fetching man. His face was always tanned perfectly by the sun, which accentuated his straight white teeth and thick white hair. He had very few freckles. His once-blue eyes were now old and turned rather a handsome gray. His hair was straight and full but lacked the color of its youthful-brassy red. It was usually parted on the side and he neatly combed it like a small boy posing for his fourth-grade school picture. A small, wild cowlick in the back always needed attention. His mother was constantly licking her fingers and trying to keep it down when he was a boy. He was still boyish at heart. Even the neatly trimmed goatee of coarse white hair couldn't conceal his little-boy smile. That smile. He was sure that's what Addy had fallen in love with first, and he'd used it to his advantage. He lay on the couch, half sleeping, half agonizing.

Between the dreams and restless awakenings, Red began to inventory his surroundings. Survival tactics, he could deal with. How or why he was cast into this new world, he was unsure about. He had a good supply of food and clothing inside the house and a garage full of tools, guns, and ammo. There was a small gas-powered generator that he used as a backup for his water well when the winter storms knocked out the power. But first things first. He needed to go find Addy, his family, and would leave as soon as he could see morning's light.

CHAPTER 3

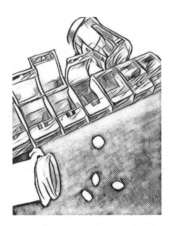

The darkness was unbearable. Each new noise drove him to the nearest window. Someone was watching. The backlight from the lantern made him feel vulnerable, but it was too dark without it. His eyes were heavy with sleep. His mind ceased to rest. How would he look for Addy? *A backpack.* He would take a backpack. *How far?* As far as his legs would take him. But he could barely get up the driveway without becoming short of breath. He felt hopeless, lost, and afraid. It was too much for him to endure. He told God he was sorry. "I don't know what I've ever done, but I'm sorry. So very sorry." The lantern was off, and darkness again commanded the room.

Red abruptly sat up. He strained to hear what sounded like a cry. A distant moan. Maybe the wind. It was near midnight when the crying began again. It always seemed darker in the mountains. Tonight was no different. The flashlight beam had grown weaker. Red moved in the direction of a sporadic whimper. He stopped several times, waiting and listening. He passed the oak and shined the light on the rear of his pickup, which was still aslant in the forest. Nothing except for the wind.

The flashlight was directed away from the truck and into the dark, colorless forest. The beam caught a reflection of a set of eyes in the blackness. Red sprung backward. He fumbled as he tried to manipulate both the flashlight and shotgun. The eyes unsteadily crept closer. With each movement, Red clumsily stepped farther backward. The light picked up more reflection and exposed the shape and color of the beast. It was Jake.

Red's fear instantly transformed into disbelief. He had been given a piece of his life back. His leg muscles quivered, and his voice stuttered as he gently called out, "J-Jake."

The dog whimpered as he slowly limped forward.

Red dropped the shotgun to the ground. He slumped to his knees, hugged the dog, and wouldn't let go. "I got you now, I got you." For a moment, the dog and man became one in the blackness. Red felt the dog lean into him, resting, becoming almost limp.

By the time he'd carried the dog onto the back porch, Red had been bitten three times: twice on the arm and once on his face. He placed Jake on the porch rug at the back-door step. He relit the lantern and lightly touched the dog's shoulder where a large patch of hair was missing. The bare skin was torn and bloodied. Red knew the dog's labored breathing, distended abdomen, and blood loss were grave. He was thankful Addy was gone. A black marking crossed over the dog's shoulder, down his back, and over his thigh. It was a tire mark. "My God, boy, you've been run over by a car." Jake was almost lifeless, and Red could tell he was in terrible pain. He wondered how the dog was still alive and couldn't bear to watch him suffer.

Red retrieved a pistol. He stood above the dog and pointed the barrel at Jake's head. He focused on the gun's sights and blocked out the view of its target. Two hands could not steady the gun. He tightly gritted his teeth as if to garner his last bit of muscle control. The dog kept looking right at him and chose not to blink. His eyes gave permission and granted forgiveness. Red held his breath. He felt his finger tighten around the trigger. Thoughts of the past blasted into his mind. The memory was fresh and clear.

Red was inside the house when he noticed Addy's car coming up the driveway. It was a hot summer's day, and she was late. It sounded as if she were in a hurry as the car skidded to a stop. The door slammed loudly, and then another door slammed. Red walked toward the kitchen door to meet her. He could hear her fast-paced high-heeled steps on the redwood decking. The back door flew open. Addy wobbled inside, trying to keep her balance while holding an oversize puppy in her arms. The pup, maybe close to a year old, was so big Red could see he must have weighed at least fifty or sixty pounds. He was a dirty, furry, depressing yellow-red lump of dog, and Addy looked furious. Red didn't dare move but managed to say, "What is that?"

Addy looked directly at Red and commanded, "He is our dog, and you will like him." Red didn't move. There was no discussion to be had. He knew it. Any objections would be futile. Addy stomped into the bathroom, placed the dog in the tub, and slammed the door. The sound of the water filling the bath muffled her conversation with the dog.

Red could hear her crying through the closed door as the bathwater splashed about. He leaned in and listened to his wife talk to the dog. "Everything is going to be just fine. You have a wonderful place to live now, where you can run and play. And wait until you meet Fang down the street. He's a little rough around the edges, but aren't all bloodhounds? You will be loved, I can assure you. Why, I love you already."

Red knew the dog would be theirs forever. There was no question about it. Within those few short moments, he stood there and fell in love with Addy all over again. If she had brought home an elephant, Red would've gladly kept it.

Red placed his forehead on the outside of the closed door and said reassuringly, "I like him, honey."

It wasn't until months later that Red learned that Addy had witnessed the dog, tied to a tree, being beaten by its owner. Addy had confronted the man, who was twice her size, and negotiated options of either calling the police or calling her husband. She then paid him three hundred dollars cash for his unwanted, unkempt, good-for-nothing dog.

Red placed the pistol down. In his lifetime, he'd dispatched many suffering animals, but he couldn't kill this one, not the only thing left of his previous life. He would let him die peacefully at home. Red cried. He carried Jake inside and laid him near the fire. He placed a tramadol down Jake's throat and squeezed water from a cloth into the dog's mouth. He retrieved Addy's crocheted throw from the couch. It smelled like Addy, so Jake would have peace. There was nothing more the man could do but keep him calm and warm.

The dog was quiet and took in only a small amount of water during the rest of the night. Red thought about Jake. How could he have been hit by a car? How did he appear a day later on this side of the world? Red wanted the night to be over. He lay down upon the couch and watched the dog's shallow breaths.

Jake was probably a mix of Labrador, Newfoundland, chow, and German shepherd. The dog didn't walk but rather pranced around with oversize feet. He knew he was beautiful and used it to his advantage. Addy could never quite get Red to give the dog more than an occasional pat on the head. But that was Jake's doing. She always believed that, until someone had loved an animal, part of their soul remained unawakened. Red liked the dog. The dog just didn't like him.

Addy liked a clean house, but she liked the hound even more. She'd wipe the dog's paws with a towel, one by one, before allowing him inside. He had designated areas, but they were rarely enforced. He was a smart dog that had a good understanding of the English language. Arithmetic, though, was harder. Jake could only count to three, a skill Addy had unintentionally taught him, as she'd done with her children. He would be unresponsive until the count of three. At "one," he would be mildly interested. At "two," he would start to pay attention, and at "three," he would come prancing over to Addy. Jake would lift his front legs high in the air with each step, leaving enough clearance for his big paws to flop forward without tripping himself.

He was a self-taught dog when it came to telling time. Each day at precisely 4:45 in the afternoon, he'd walk down to the end of the drive and wait for Addy to get home from work. She would stop, open her car door, and let the big mutt jump across her lap and ride shotgun all the way back up the drive. He loved Addy. He hated cats, other dogs, and Red. He had the disposition of a cat trapped in the body of a dog.

Now Jake was the only living reminder of, and maybe even the answer to, Red's new world. He prayed for the dog's life.

At morning's first light, the dog was still alive, asleep in front of the fire. Nothing appeared to be broken, and Red was thankful. "Hey, buddy, looks like we're in this together. Let me have a look." He carefully applied salve to the dog's shoulder and told him everything was going to be OK. He took an oversize T-shirt and placed the dog's head through the neck of the shirt and a front leg in each of the armholes and tied the hem around Jake's belly. It would keep the dog from licking his wounds. "It's better than a cone," Red said aloud.

The dog whimpered but submitted. Red walked away and allowed the dog to go back to sleep.

As Jake slept quietly now, Red tended to his own wounds. He turned on the faucet, only to be reminded his world had changed. No water. "Idiot." He looked at his disheveled clothing. After being slightly disabled by a hunting accident years ago, he'd slowed down. When he was tired, he walked with a visible limp. He had been a real estate broker and had even introduced Addy to and tutored her on running the family business. Addy was good, very good. Financially, it allowed Red time away for hunting and fishing. But, as of late, he had abdicated all decision-making to Addy, except for the occasional times at the grocery store: paper or plastic. His eyes blurred as he stared at his reflection, remembering another time.

Red combed through his thick white hair with aging hands in the same mirror. He leaned forward, closer to the mirror, and touched the wrinkles around his eyes. Addy's soft hands came around him from behind. He looked at her reflection peering out from behind him. She smiled and hugged him as he leaned against the sink.

"I don't know why you put up with me. I'm a wrinkly old man."

Addy pulled him tighter and spoke softly into his ear. "We've earned those wrinkles together, and I wouldn't trade them for anything."

Red inspected his neck. "Well, I guess I still have hair. I should be thankful for that." He tugged on his white goatee and looked at his teeth. "And I got my teeth."

Addy laughed. "You certainly do, and if you didn't, I'd still be in love with you."

"You love everyone, including a dog that hates me."

"Jake's gotten better with age," she said as she nudged Red from in front of the mirror. "Just like you." Addy quickly adjusted her hair, kissed Red on the cheek, and left the room.

Red centered himself in front of the mirror again and said, "I've got liver spots, too."

Addy's voice came from the bedroom: "You're fine, I love your spots as well. Now take your pills. And, besides, in dog years, you're only nine."

He wanted Addy back. Red looked at his reflection. *How did I get so old, so fast? Where did all the years go?* He tucked in his shirttail, retrieved his handgun, and went outside. The day was clear but crisp. Autumn was in the air. Leaves rustled in the trees high above. He stopped at the oak tree and picked up the shotgun he had dropped during the night. He walked the perimeter of the truck and looked for tire marks, skids, debris, or anything else that might have helped explain how Jake had been injured. There was nothing. Had Jake come through a secret doorway? Red turned toward the forest, held up his opened hand in the air in front of him, and spread his fingers apart. He wanted to find the passageway, the passageway that had returned Jake. He needed to feel a puff of warm air or see his hand wane into another dimension pulling him back into reality.

Red tended to Jake for the rest of the day and throughout the night. Jake's breathing had improved, but he was unable to stand without help. The confused dog defecated on the carpet and himself, but Red didn't care. "It's OK, Jake, it's all right." He cleaned the dog first and gave him another fresh blanket for his bedding. He partially wrapped the blanket around the dog. "There, see? She'll never know. It's our secret. Our secret between us boys."

Red cleaned up the carpet. He would leave the house and search for Addy and his family as soon as Jake could be left alone. Jake whimpered off and on. "Just stay still, boy. I'm here. We're in this together now."

CHAPTER 4

To the west about a mile or so, there'd been a main road from Paradise to Stirling City called the Skyway. It ran north and south on top of a finger ridge just above the snow line. There, Red would find Addy at her brother's house waiting for him and wondering what had taken him so long. Red packed his backpack. Instead of the shotgun, he picked a .30-06 Weatherby from the gun rack. He loaded the rifle and put the rest of the shells in his pants pocket. Jake was left sequestered in the house with plenty of water.

The gravel driveway still stopped at the same old oak tree, with Pollux and Castor standing sentry near the property line. At the oak, Red turned north and started to pick his way through the forest. Navigation and bearings had always been simple. But things would be different now. Red knew that if he got lost he would be lost forever, and no one would ever know. His mother always told him, "If you ever get lost, just follow the first creek down. Sooner or later, a bridge will cross the creek, and you can follow the road until you run into some folks." He actually thought he heard his mother's voice. He knew it was hers, but it sounded younger.

"OK, Momma, I sure will."

Generally, the terrain was downhill from where he'd started all the way to the creek, which flowed through the old Sam Vandegrift ranch. A small spring saturated the ground, making it soggy and spongy. Red examined some animal prints. They had to be from elk. It would be hard to mistake those tracks. It was uncanny, as elk had not been this low or in this county for a hundred years.

Red thought he felt curiosity, or maybe it was courage. He looked around at the unfamiliar forest and felt his fingers tighten around the rifle. No, it was not curiosity or courage. He was alone and scared. *I'm gonna get myself lost!* He was feeling adrenaline from fear. *Where did everything go? Why is this happening to me? I'm gonna have a heart attack. I have to slow down. Breathe, just breathe. I'll find Addy. I'll wake up and all will be OK. This is a nightmare.* He wiped the sweat from his forehead. "Slow down. Just slooow down."

Red finally reached the creek and drank the cool water from his cupped hand. The creek led him to Vandegrift's meadow and pond. He stood at the pond's edge and watched hundreds of fish bob to the surface, in numbers he'd never seen before. They thrived like koi in the small pond, fighting for space.

A small knoll sat at the edge of the forest, overlooking most of the meadow. He surveyed his surroundings, and his gaze stopped on a big bull elk. An oversize set of antlers sat precariously upon its regal head. The beast and the man were thirty short yards from one another. The bull chewed its cud, looked at the man, and showed no fear. After scanning the human, the bull slowly meandered into the forest and disappeared.

The creature shouldn't have been there. Red looked down at the meadow, past where the bull had been standing, and saw circles of crushed grass, evidence of where the bull and his harem had bedded down. He glassed over the area with his rifle scope and stopped on a spot north of the meadow. A large pond with a beaver's dam filled the area. The regenerated wildlife was shocking.

Elk, now beaver, but no houses. I must be crazy. He shook his head, searching for a way to make sense of what he was seeing. Nothing was logical. He wondered if he were in another dimension and, more importantly, how he could get back to the right one.

Red cut across the meadow to the west. He continued until reaching the edge of Butte Creek Canyon, well past where the roadway should have been. But there was nothing but trees. In the past, the forest had bequeathed comfort, like the lulling of ocean waves, consistent, faithful, and forgiving. But now, the woodland had betrayed him, swallowing up everything he'd ever loved. The once-inviting forest now craved even more. It had become a suffocating shroud, sucking oxygen from the air until there was none. He screamed out for Addy as the forest squeezed tighter. He needed to see blue sky. The green canopy encased him from above. The once-soft ferns on the forest floor turned into creeping tentacles, wrapping themselves around his legs and pulling him down. "Addy!" He cupped his hands around his mouth and screamed out again, "Addy!"

He was sure he was standing where a neighborhood should've been. Addy would be at the yellow house, second on the left, directly down the street. There should've been cars and streetlamps. People should've been using their mowers or blowing leaves from their yards. People jogging, walking their dogs, kids riding bikes. Charlotte should've been delivering the mail.

He retraced his steps to the beaver pond. As he walked past the dam, he saw fresh prints cast in the mud. They were the largest bear tracks he had ever seen. He knelt down and placed his hand next to the indentation. It was bigger than both of his hands put together. It had to be the print of a grizzly bear. He immediately stood, gripped his rifle, and brought it to his chest.

Red had been a hunter all his life but had never seen a grizzly outside of the Sacramento Zoo. He cautiously picked his way back to the knoll. From the top of the rise, he continued to track the bear's path through the scope until it went out of sight behind the pond. He methodically followed his own trail homeward while trying to watch for the bear. His nerves were raw. He jumped at every little movement or noise. He could feel an aura about him, a sensation of something sinister. Had he actually gone back in time? An unwitting time traveler cast into an era before man. But now, Addy was home, waiting. Matthew and Sam must be with her, worried sick. They'd all be crying, even Matthew. He must be so afraid. He was the man of the family now. Red squinted tears from his eyes, too afraid to loosen the grip on his gun.

Forty-five minutes later, Red was back in his driveway. He rested against the big oak. He saw the house through the trees and lowered his head in relief. Only then did he allow himself to realize how out of shape he had become as he plodded up the drive.

Jake was up on his feet and met him at the door wearing the John Deere T-shirt.

"Don't look at me that way. You're better off in here. Trust me."

The dog growled, got a drink from the water bowl, and limped back to his bed.

Red was exhausted. Necessary chores took him twice as long as they should have. He started a fire in the backyard firepit and put on a pot of stew. He filled up the tub in the master bath and would use the water to refill the toilet reservoir.

When he finished the washing, he looked in the mirror. Except for the dog bite, he saw the same familiar face looking back at him that he had seen for so many years. Cleaning up a bit made him feel better but also made him wonder how he could have taken so many things for granted—a hot shower being one of them.

There were some things Red had to do right away. There were still four hours or so of daylight. He hauled the meat from the garage freezer into the kitchen and started making jerky. He placed meat strips into a washtub, added his brine, and covered it with a big beach towel to keep off the flies.

As Red picked up the big cast-iron pot of stew, the handle broke away, and its entire contents spilled into the fire. Steam burst up from the coals, and Red was left holding an empty, broken-handled pot as the dog watched from the open back door. The firepit vehemently consumed the stew. Nothing was salvageable. Red kicked at the firepit. "I christen you Dante in the name of the Father, Son, and Holy Ghost. Baptized in stew."

Jake whined and returned to the living room. Red watched the steam rise. "I wasn't hungry anyway, you bastard."

Red tried to sleep. He needed the rest, but his mind wouldn't stop. Entire neighborhoods had vanished without a trace. Roads were gone. Communication was impossible. His house and property were the only evidence of mankind that had been spared. "What the hell do I do now?" The darkness didn't answer. *I guess I survive and prepare. I've got to find my family. But I've got to stay alive to do so.*

Both man and dog were up before the sun. Red checked on the vat of brine and meat. Then he made small S-hooks using wire from coat hangers that he'd bought at a garage sale last year. Five hundred of them for a penny a piece. Addy had laughed at him when he'd told her what a bargain they'd been. He skewered the meat strips onto the hooks, then hung them on a line he had strung across the backyard.

Jake was healing amazingly well and seemed ready for a short venture out of the backyard. He was slow but obviously wanted to go. He wasn't yet strong enough to be left alone for more than a few hours, and Red was pretty sure Addy would want his priority to be Jake, for now. Red picked up his shotgun and followed behind, letting his limping dog take the lead. It'd been their backyard for years, but every game trail, logging skid road, and man-made marker, once thoroughly familiar, was replaced with a deep and unacquainted woodland.

The forest's canopy diffused the sunlight. The woodland was oddly beautiful. Red followed Jake into a clearing just ahead. The colors of fall illuminated the meadow. Leaves danced in the wind while enjoying their descent to the earth. The rustling of a nearby aspen's bright-yellow foliage attracted his attention. The leaves twisted in the wind, exposing both front and back, from sheen to dull, making them twinkle with sunlight like flickering night-lights. A burst of wind freed a handful of leaves and cast them outward until they glittered out of sight. Aspen had never grown so close to Red's home.

A dogwood's ruby foliage backlit the yellow aspen. Addy loved the fall. She always harvested branches from the forest dogwoods, putting their twigs of yellow, orange, red, and maroon in glass vases. The magical arrangements breathed life to the indoors. It was her way, her little secret, for prolonging the fall for as long as she could.

Red walked to the dogwood. "My God, look at this, Jake. It's massive." Compared to the five- or six-inch-diameter dogwood trees that existed in his old world, this dogwood was impossibly giant.

"This is what Addy was always talking about. The beauty of Vermont in the fall." Red's memory was clear.

Addy came into the house, her face partially covered by green boughs and autumn dogwood branches. "Red, just look how beautiful. This makes me want to go back home all over again."

"Home? This is your home." Red didn't even put down the newspaper he was reading.

"No, Red, back home to Vermont. I just don't understand why you don't want to go visit."

"It's not that I don't want to. We just don't have the time. That's a long way away."

Addy fussed with the arrangement in the kitchen sink. "You're retired. What else do you have to do?"

"It's cold back there."

"It's not cold, it's autumn."

"It's humid, and who would take care of Jake?"

"Jake? You're suddenly concerned for Jake now? You know that Matt or Sam would love to take Jake for a couple days."

The memory was fresh and made Red feel annoyed with himself. *What an ass.*

The sun had crossed the tops of the trees, and soon it would be getting dark. Red called out to Jake, but it garnered no response. The dog's hearing was fine, but his loyalty was not. He must have forgotten his arithmetic, because that did not work, either. Red counted again, this time getting to seven. *Seven.* A memory burst into his mind.

A young girl opened the front door and allowed him to step inside.

"You must be Sam?" Red asked.

She stood firm in front of him as he nervously sat down on the hard sofa and waited for Addy, her mom. Red cleared his throat and prepared for the confrontation.

"You're not my father," she said matter-of-factly.

"No. I can never be your father." Red thought maybe the denial would ease the tension. He was wrong. At this point, it would prove useless to explain his intentions. Her eyes were fixed. Her pigtails were as tight as her folded arms.

"Grandmother said that Mr. Delhanson at the bank said you're at least good with numbers."

Red conjured a seemingly polite smile with a single nod.

"What's the square root of forty-nine?"

There were exactly three things that would happen now. One, he could answer incorrectly and the interrogation from the nine-year-old would be over. Two, he could continue with the correct answer and be subjected to additional inquiries. Or, three, he could leave while he was still in one piece.

"Seven."

"What's a hundred forty-four times twelve divided by two?"

Are you kidding me? My pending social life depends on a mathematics quiz proctored by a four-foot rapscallion? He wanted to clear his throat, but that was surely a dead giveaway of his nervousness.

"Eight hundred sixty-four." *Please let that be correct.*

One step forward with her arms down straight now, eyes almost to a squint.

"What are the four points of the compass?"

"Cardinal or intercardinal?" There, he had her. Would it be enough to disarm? Break the ice? Open the door? Or had it been too snide?

"Do you know anything about celestial navigation?"

"Nope."

"Dead reckoning?"

"Now you're scaring me."

"You're still not my father, and you'll never be my father. He loves me more than anything." Sam turned and started to walk away.

"I don't blame him. He must be pretty special to you."

She paused and turned slightly. "He said I can have a dog now. And he's gonna get me one as soon as he gets back." This time, her voice was a little less challenging.

"Really? That's so exciting! Why, I think I have an extra brush. Let's see, maybe a collar, too. Yep, your dad must really love you," Red said with a genuine smile.

Red called out to Jake two more times. Finally, the dog turned and started walking toward the man. "Well, all right, then. Get over here." In reality, the dog hadn't obeyed but rather had just changed his mind and wanted to go home. Red felt better with the company, but Jake was indifferent.

Red was tired of sleeping on the couch and decided that both he and Jake would sleep in the bedroom. It would be the first night Red hadn't slept in his clothes. The bed was comforting. He reached down and started to pet Jake, who was curled up on the rug. Jake interrupted the moment by walking into the living room. Red looked at the empty pillow next to him. He missed his wife and moved to her side of the bed. He held her pillow close to his face, breathed in the smell of her hair, and fell asleep. He wanted to be with her, he wanted to feel again. When could he have his life back?

The darkness broke with shrill, unrestrained barking. Jake ran back and forth from the bedroom sliding glass door to the bed in a frenzy to get outside. Red jumped from bed and groped for the flashlight. He felt Jake's teeth sink deep into his leg. Red screamed in pain and fell to the floor. The commotion outside was nearly as loud as the chaos inside. Jake attacked the glass door. He stood on his hind feet, placing his front paws high upon the glass, scratching and biting, growling and barking. He clawed at the glass and would not stop under anyone's command. He stood over six feet tall. Red shined the light at the glass, but the reflection lit only the inside. He limped in closer. The window blind was halfway torn away and wrapped around Jake. He worried that the dog would break the glass and managed to grab Jake's collar and gain some control. Finally, the barking assaults turned to low, continuous snarls.

Red didn't feel the coldness on his bare skin. He checked the lock on the door but couldn't process his racing thoughts. He checked it again. He peered through the glass door and worked the flashlight back and forth. He knew the light made him a target, but it was safer than opening the door. His breath fogged the glass. He quickly wiped it away and cupped his eyes again. He was afraid. Too afraid to go out into his own backyard and investigate.

He'd become a scared little boy who'd been left alone at home for the first time. His instructions were to never open the door. Monsters were under the bed, waiting to attack. He wanted to be found in a game of hide-and-seek, hiding deep in the closet beneath the clothes. He wanted to be rescued. He wanted a rescinding hand to pull him back to his once-safe life. He wanted law and order. His naked body made him feel vulnerable, helpless.

The scared old man sat in the dark and held on to his calf muscle while Jake recused himself to the living room like nothing had happened. This was not unusual behavior for the dog. Red himself had been victim to Jake's attacks through the glass door. But this time, the dog's size and power were comforting. Red would wait until morning to go outside. Maybe he could find tracks or prints. Maybe determine whether it was man or beast. Or alien.

Red lit the lantern and nursed his throbbing leg. Blood oozed from the puncture wound: one deep hole from the canine tooth, the rest superficial tears. His leg muscle ached deep inside with burning coldness. A large scar stretched from his hip to his knee. He rubbed the atrophied muscle beneath the line of smooth taunt skin on the old wound. His hand would sometimes go there automatically when he thought about the accident. It always ached during the winter months and definitely hurt more than the dog bite.

He put on his clothes and returned to the door. He shined the flashlight through the glass. The jerky meat was gone, along with the entire line! It had been strung high between the trees, so what on earth could have taken it? Maybe that was the issue. *Maybe I'm not on earth anymore.* He turned off the light, and all was black again. Maybe he wasn't on earth anymore. He slept on the couch with his shotgun while Jake slept peacefully in Addy's leather chair. As Red lay in quiet darkness, he wanted to pray to God but couldn't muster a voice. Maybe he really didn't want to talk to God anyway. God had taken away his family. But God wasn't supposed to punish.

The next morning, Red replayed the night's events in his head. He put fresh batteries in the flashlight, then duct-taped it to the barrel of the shotgun. He raised and lowered the gun several times. He didn't want to have any repeat performances of the previous night's disaster.

Red tended to his new wound, along with the dog's old injuries. As he removed Jake's T-shirt and bandage, he expected to find fresh blood, maybe infection. However, the wound was dry and almost healed. He put his hand on the dog's side and felt the wound in disbelief. "That's crazy. How could it heal so quickly?"

Red stood up sharply and stared down at his dog. *Time. I must have lost track of the time. It would have taken weeks for that to heal. I need to write down the days. I need to keep track. I'm in fast-forward.* "This is insane."

CHAPTER 5

His home was seven miles above the town of Paradise and twenty-eight miles from Chico. Fifteen or so miles down the Skyway, and he'd be able to see the city of Chico from Lookout Point. On a clear day, he could see the entire Sacramento Valley. He wanted to go. He wanted to see if other towns were gone, too. He would not give up until he found answers. He'd have to sleep outside at night, and that scared him to death. It was a real wilderness now, deep and dark with unknown inhabitants.

The dog seemed to recognize the familiar routine of packing. He followed the man back and forth from the garage to the kitchen. Red packed the supplies in a small backpack. It was eleven in the morning before Red was ready. He packed supplies to last four or five days, along with his shotgun and .22 rifle for protection and hunting.

Jake was ready. Thick red hair had grown back some over the wound, but it was still lighter and shorter next to the rest of his long, soft coat, making it look like he had a severe case of the mange. His limp was gone, replaced with attitude. Jake would have to assist this time, carrying a light load. Red fitted Jake with a nylon canine saddle-bag. The dog was less than impressed. He fussed with the pack, nipping and pulling, then finally rolling on his back. With the house locked, Red placed the key over the door, and the two marauders began their journey.

Coutolenc Road used to follow a long ridge to the south. His goal for the day was to reach a small plateau on top of the canyon ridge near the small community of Old Magalia. The high point would give him a clear view of distant landmarks.

Both man and dog had to stop and rest frequently. Game trails were everywhere, crossing the ridge and going to or coming from the creeks on either side. Red was taken aback at the quantity of deer and elk tracks. Sawmill Peak was in clear view, but there were no signs of the Forest Service fire lookout station that had once been perched at the top of the peak.

Red spotted a covey of grouse roosting in a small pine tree. He always had called them "fool hens." Grouse had been rare in California for a hundred years and could only be found in the high country. And even there, he'd only seen one bunch in twenty years' time.

Red took aim with his .22 rifle. He remembered how, when they were young boys, his brother had taught him to shoot the bottom bird first. He heard his brother's whisper, "If you shoot the top bird, it'll fall right through the other birds and scare 'em all away."

He hadn't thought of his older brother in years. He wanted to live that simple life again. To be carefree and have someone else guide his life and keep him safe. If he could just do it all over, things would be different. George and Red had been inseparable children of the forties, children of an unwitting circumstance.

Red remembered the flat, cold high country and could almost smell the wetness of the sage and juniper trees.

George leaned in over his younger brother's shoulder, almost taking aim himself, and said, "Tuck it into your shoulder, squeeze easy now." The barrel of the .22 rested against the bark of a juniper tree.

George was five years older than Red and naturally watched over his younger brother.

Young Red closed his left eye, took aim, closed his other eye, and yanked on the trigger. The shot missed.

"Red, you gotta keep both eyes open no matter what, and you gotta squeeze easy." George saw the disappointment in Red's face and said, "Come on, we'll find some more, and you can get 'em then."

As the two boys walked, the smaller asked, "Why doesn't Momma like guns?"

"Don't be such an idiot, Red. Wasn't she happy when we brought home that big ol' turkey, and what about the last little buck? Remember, we all stayed up all night and fixed it into jerky?"

Red nodded. "Yeah, I guess so."

The sound of Jake barking brought Red back from his daydream. Red quickly pulled the trigger before the birds could fly away. He killed three and tied them on the top of his pack.

By the time he'd reached the plateau, the sun was setting behind a dark skyline of silhouetted pines. Red stood on the ridge plateau between the sunset and Sawmill Peak and watched the mountaintop reap in the last of the sunlight.

Red cleared a spot for his sleeping bag. He was surrounded by a native grove of MacNab cypress trees. The fire-resistant trees looked like miniature coastal cypress, but instead of thriving in soft, sandy soil, as their cousins did, the MacNabs made their hard living through the shimmering green serpentinite rock. *Strange trees,* he thought as he lay on his back. He reached upward and plucked a limb from the tree and smelled its branchlet. Its powerful aroma smelled of Christmas. The branchlet was dotted with tiny glandular pits that sparkled like the serpentinite rock itself.

He threw the branch into the fire. As the flames touched the branchlets, short bursts of air pushed the fire away. It snapped and popped like a line of distant firecrackers. He picked up one of the discarded cypress cones on the ground and examined it. He picked up another, then, quickly, another. Maybe because of the backlighting from the fire, he now noticed their unusual shape. When he turned the cones just right, they each resembled a head with devil horns.

"The fireproof devil himself."

The dark silence was broken by the whine of mosquitoes. They were nasty little things that sang their nasty little songs. He kept the fire going but often thought the flames just seemed to emphasize the darkness. Jake was indifferent to the situation and chose to sleep on his side of the campsite.

Red woke at first light, packed up his camp, and made sure the fire was out. They climbed a small hill through towering pines and firs to a flat spot on the edge of the canyon. His eyes analyzed the area. Yes, this was the spot. The Old Magalia church was well over one hundred years old, but now, it'd vanished along with the entire cemetery.

Red dropped his backpack and frantically scanned the ground beneath him. Back and forth, quickly kicking up dirt with the toe of his boot. He stepped to a new spot and did the same. This was where the cemetery had been, right there under his feet. Red fell to his knees. His fingers desperately clawed at the ground, ripping at the dirt like an animal digging for its cornered prey. God wouldn't have taken the dead, decaying remnants lying dormant for years. What kind of monster would have invaded such hallowed ground, disturbing such sacredness with ravaged heartlessness? His fingertips bled as his nails broke away.

He thrust his bowie knife into the earth, penetrating deeply. The blade shredded through the grasses and soil, inch after inch. His eyes brimmed with tears that fell straight down to the earth, leaving no trace upon his face. It was hopeless. He held the knife in both hands as he leaned backward. His scream was silent, no one was there to hear it. He was alone and empty. Even the dead were gone, maybe even God.

A large boulder provided a chair where he sat and listened to familiar sounds—all kinds of ducks, mallards, sprig, and widgeon quacking, peeping, and whistling right over his head. He'd heard those sounds every spring and fall for as long as he had lived in Paradise.

He watched a young spike buck in a small clearing not far ahead. They were close enough to one another to make eye contact. The buck watched as the man slowly raised his rifle. Red was shaking from fatigue. He rested the rifle barrel against a tree and pulled the trigger.

He'd forgotten to bring a deer sack to wrap up the harvested meat. He removed his white undershirt, wrapped the meat, and put it in the pack. He had to leave the front quarters behind. In the past, he would have utilized nearly every scrap. He stood over the discarded remains. Never had he killed an animal and left it to rot. He felt strange, as if he had poached the animal out of season or for sport. He needed meat, he needed to eat. It wasn't his choice to be thrust into a new world of unknowns, and playing by old rules was foolish.

He followed the ridge down southward until he came upon a small spring somewhere south of Magalia. He was no longer surprised to see elk tracks. He gathered some firewood, cleared off a space, and started a fire. After it had burned down to a good bed of coals, he put one of the backstraps on the small grill and ate his dinner.

The sun was warm, and it was easy to fall asleep during the daylight hours. He must've been asleep for nearly an hour when Jake's growling woke him up. A small herd of elk had come to the spring. Jake crashed out after the elk with the passion of a young dog. Red struggled to get to his feet as quickly as he wanted to. The herd disappeared over the ridge with Jake following closely behind. "Jake! No!" He was afraid Jake wouldn't return. In the new world, he felt isolated, but without the dog, he would be alone for sure. He waited for Jake and called out to him several times. Finally, Jake appeared in the distance, tired and thirsty.

Red tried to follow where the Skyway used to traverse through the middle of the town of Paradise. A large boulder protruded from the ground. A sight to behold. Red knew exactly where he was now. Billie Park! This had been the site of an old homestead, a large ranch with fruit trees and olive orchards. But all of that was gone. He climbed to the top of the boulder. It was a well-known landmark, documented in local history and linked to the Maidu Indians, who'd used it for grinding food. The boulder was the same, except there were no grinding holes or any signs of wear. He touched the stone with his hand where the holes and depressions should have been. He nervously looked around and slowly backed away. He wanted to scream.

CHAPTER 6

Red followed the canyon's edge with Jake trailing in the distance. From there, he could see all the way to the coastal range. Within the faraway blue mountains, he easily made out Tomhead Mountain and Anthony Peak, even though they were fifty or sixty miles across the basin.

This was the perfect spot to see the largest portion of Butte Creek Canyon. Red looked through his binoculars, hoping to see radio towers, roads, or the houses that once filled the canyon. But there was nothing.

Lookout Point, several miles down the ridge, would provide the next check of the valley. At night, surely he could see the lights of neighboring communities. "One small light is all that I need."

It'd been one of Red's fantasies to see the Sacramento Valley before it had been so populated and polluted by man. Funny, he was now living that fantasy. Game was abundant, the earth was pristine, and he could walk upon land never before touched by any man. He started to smile, then stopped. He'd gotten his wish at the cost of his family. He slowly closed his eyes and breathed in deeply. He felt Jake by his side and reached down and touched his head. "Be careful what you wish for, Jake."

It was late in the afternoon, and he was tired. He recalled a small creek about a mile away. He found it surrounded by brush and blackberry bushes. He filled both his and Jake's water jugs and hiked up a small hill.

He made camp while Jake rested nearby. Red wrinkled up his nose, squinted, and looked at the dog. "Good God, you stink. You're offensive." He continued to badger the dog while starting a fire. "You damn well know that Addy would be furious with you. And me! She'd be furious at me for letting you get that way." He sat down away from the dog, smelled his underarms, pulled the front of his shirt up to his nose, and sniffed. "Good Lord." He had not taken a bath in several days. His backpack reeked of decomposing death from carrying the bloodied undershirt. He took himself, the backpack, shirt, and dog back down to the creek. The water was cold, but it felt good on his overused muscles.

The creek was full of trout. Red was already in the water, so he decided fish was an excellent dinner choice. He kept the dog away from the water and found several small pools overflowing with trout. He was able to catch three by "tickling" their bellies. Their bodies were firm and plump. They had that delicate, familiar smell of just-caught wild rainbow trout. He and his brother had caught fish the same way. He remembered how he and George used to skip school on the unbearably hot days. Neither cared much for school anyway. He saw two blue-eyed, shirtless boys with tanned skin and white teeth. They'd escaped down a dusty cow path, through old lady Wilcox's pasture.

Both boys discarded their tattered shoes and socks and stepped into the water. George had made a pollywog catcher out of a metal can attached to a stick. The bottom of the can was pierced full of nail holes, a sieve for chasing after the elusive polliwog or minnows. In turn, the detainees were used as bait to catch the bigger fish. Sometimes, Red chose a lucky pollywog, took it home, and tended it safely into a grand frog. Red netted a handful of minnows before losing his balance. He dropped the can, spilling the contents back into the creek.

"It's OK, Red. We'll just take out the middleman and catch the fish with our hands."

Bent over and arms stretched outward, they herded fish to the shallower pools of water. "All we have to do, Red, is tickle their bellies, and they won't be able to move."

"Ya just gotta herd them up under the rocks like this. Let them think they're hiding in the shade behind the boulders." He put both hands under the water. "Feel their bellies and slowly move your hand up like this. Listen. You can almost hear 'em laughin' right now."

Red adjusted his head and listened.

"Then feel up to just about their gills and squeeze."

Red watched intently until George's hands burst up out of the water. Empty. Then again. Empty. "It doesn't look like it's working, George."

On the third try, George's hands burst out of the water clasping a squirming fish! George held the fish out toward his little brother and hollered with joy. "See there, look at this one, Red!" He carefully transferred it into his little brother's hands.

Red proudly attached it to a forked stick and dangled it in the water at the creek's edge.

The memory made him smile. They had been a team, never to part. After all, they had promised. He made a skewer from a forked stick cut from a nearby willow branch. The blackberry vines still produced plump, juicy berries. As he plucked and gathered the fruits into his hat, their smell reminded him of the pies and jams his mother used to make. He roasted the trout, head and tail included, over the open fire. Jake wanted nothing to do with the fish entrée and opted for a piece of the deer ham.

The forested camp grew dark, and Red reminisced about days spent with his brother. George would have been proud of his catch earlier that day. He closed his eyes and thought about his brother again.

After leaving the creek, the two boys remained together for the rest of the afternoon. George bragged about how he was going to fry up all thirteen fish, smother them in ketchup, and eat them all.

"George, you gotta share with me. Just one, just let me eat one?"

"Well, I'll tell you what. I could use your help. I'll let you clean 'em, and if ya do a good job, well, I'll let you have the biggest one all to yourself."

Young Red smiled. Of course, he could help out.

As they headed for home, they crossed through the quiet little town. The local storekeeper at the general store, Mr. McAdams, admired the catch. "Well, I could rightly sell those fish to my customers." He offered a penny apiece, but with George's marketing skills, Mr. McAdams reluctantly agreed to a nickel per fish and gave them each a cold soda pop to boot.

We're rich! The boys ran and hid in the forest at the edge of town. George cleared out a spot on the ground and laid out all the coins on his handkerchief. There were two quarters and fifteen pennies. The boys huddled over their treasure.

"Red, we're gonna split this fair and square, but since you tied up all them fish and did all that work, I'm gonna give ya a choice."

Young Red nodded his head in excitement. "OK, OK. I worked real hard. What are we gonna do?" Red knew George had always been fair with people his whole life. He depended on George. He was his best friend, and best friends never, never cheat.

"Now, look here, you can have your choice between fifteen of these pretty copper pennies, or only two of these clumsy old silver ones."

Young Red thought, bit his lip, and said, "Well, stringin' all them wiggly fish was really hard—I'll take all those pretty ones."

It was the first time in days that Red fell asleep happy. But now, he dreamt through different eyes. He felt as if he were a voyeur in his own dream.

The boys took their coins and soda pop before Mr. McAdams could renege on the agreement. The screen door slammed and bounced against the doorframe as George and Red fled down the dirt road. Mr. McAdams took the stringer of fish, walked out back, and buried the fish in his vegetable garden.

"I don't know why you do that," a female voice said.

Mr. McAdams looked up, smiled, and said, "Ain't no one gonna buy them fish. Those boys need the money, and they've been raised up not to take handouts from anybody."

"You know those boys are nothing but trouble. Even their daddy couldn't handle them." The woman was now standing closer to the garden. "Are you listening to me?"

Mr. McAdams patted the top of the freshly tilled dirt with the back of the shovel. He was listening. He wanted to tell her to stop, to listen to herself, to shut up. But he was too kind of a man. "It don't hurt to help someone out, Ruth."

"You're an old fool. Someday, they'll rob us blind."

The wind had died down, and the fire was out, when Red was awakened by the morning sun. He'd slept soundly through the entire night. He wondered if what he dreamed had really happened. It seemed so real. He smiled at the thought of good ol' Mr. McAdams. But why would his wife think he would steal from her. Red had never stolen a thing in his life. He shook his head to clear away the memory, gathered his belongings, and negotiated with Jake to wear the saddlebag. "Come on, Jake. You gotta pull your own weight now. Addy would want it that way, OK?"

The two traveled slowly, stopping regularly for water and rest. The green forest gave way to the spiky Digger pine and poison oak. Red was fairly immune to poison oak, except when he occasionally contracted it from cats or dogs. Therefore, he assumed he'd have no issue. It was early afternoon before they reached Lookout Point, where Skyway used to run along the canyon's edge. He stood at the rim of the canyon and enjoyed the breeze that wafted up the side of the deep ravine. The cliff edge dropped off straight for several hundred yards.

To the southwest, the Sacramento Valley was the familiar golden color created by the curing of grasses on the valley floor. He saw the same watercourses, still easy to pick out by the tree lines that marked their winding paths southward, though the plaid patches of rice fields and orchards had vanished. The air was clear and clean as far as a human eye could see. Yes, this is what Red had always dreamt about. Pristine air and unsoiled land. But it didn't matter now. He wanted his family.

Red removed his backpack and let it drop to the ground. A kettle of vultures flew at the edge of the canyon, using the warm thermals to effortlessly go wherever they wanted. Red sniffed his armpits to see if maybe they were circling for him. He always watched buzzards with wonder. They were the ugliest of birds, with their black undertaker garb and grizzled faces, yet they were as graceful as Fred Astaire. Not even a glider pilot could duplicate the easy way they soared through the air. How he envied their flight! The man and dog stood side by side at the edge of the canyon. Jake's thick, shiny golden-red hair moved with the breeze.

"Maybe I'll come back as a buzzard." Red thought more about it. "I can work out the diet later."

He raised his rifle over his head and shot a burst of three distress shots. The echo was immediate, but he listened for more. "Please, someone hear this." He lowered the rifle and turned his back toward the cliff. Three shots rang out. He spun back around. *Were those real? They must have been!* He stared over the edge of the cliff without looking at his rifle as he filled it with more shells. He held it high. Without taking his eyes off the canyon below, he fired.

Kaboom! Kaboom! Kaboom!

For a split second, it was the loudest sound imaginable. The concussion so intense, he felt it hit his body. Three more shots returned. He raised the rifle and fired three more shots. Red kept it in the air as he awaited the return. It was not until he fired four more sets that he realized the return fire had been a strange reverberating double echo from out of the canyon. As the last empty shell casing clanked on the lava-cap ground, a crushing stillness followed. Red stood motionless. He felt raw. Abandoned.

To the west and south, the valley far below stretched out for hundreds of miles. On a clear night, it was one of the most beautiful spots in Butte County. Tens of thousands of lights would glow in the darkness, exposing positions of towns, cities, and communities spread across the three adjoining counties. Hundreds of ranches and farms to the north had dotted the canyon's bottom. Surely, if there was other human life out there, Red would see evidence from here. It would be the first time in days that he'd welcome the darkness. Each setting sun had brought with it despair and fear, magnified in irrational, dark conjectures. But, tonight, there on the point, he would wait in the darkness for hope, for his people, for his life.

The night grew darker with each passing hour, and his hope of seeing man-made light faded. If only he could spot one small light. He was sure he would see it—one, then another and another. But there was nothing. He waited for his eyes to adjust even further to the darkness. If he looked hard enough, he might see camp light from small fires and lamps. He sat near the rim of the canyon on the edge of a black noth- ingness. The moon felt distant and the stars seemed uncaring. Red sat in the darkness, refusing to start a fire. *If God wants it dark, then he can have it his way for now.*

CHAPTER 7

R ed took one last look over the canyon's edge. His eyes followed the canyon floor where a community had once existed. A lone antelope stood below. Then he saw another, then another. It was an entire herd of antelope! But antelope had not been in the valley for over 150 years!

Yet there they were.

The herd startled. Just to the north of the antelope, a great bear showed itself near an outcropping of rocks. The bear posed no threat because of the distance, but the antelope remained vigilant. Red quickly fumbled for his binoculars and confirmed the great bear was, in fact, a grizzly. Another bear bounded out of the wild grapevines and bounced into the water. Red estimated them to be five feet at the shoulders, making them eight to ten feet tall when standing upright.

The bears stalked fish in the creek ripples. Their big paws worked quickly, with skill and precision. With a fish clamped in each of their jaws, they retreated to a sandbar on the far side of the creek to devour their feast.

The scent of the bears must've spooked the antelope. Together as one, the herd ran in the opposite direction. Red had forgotten about the coordinated movement of antelope and how they flowed effortlessly and turned together as one, like a school of fish, uncertain which way to flee.

Red did not know exactly how long he stayed and watched the creatures below. His legs were stiff, and his butt was sore from sitting on the jagged lava-rock crag. The sun was directly above. It was time to go. A southern loop would add about five miles to the return home, but the walking would be easier, less strenuous. The dog took the lead, which allowed the man to secretly eat the last of the crackers he'd brought.

Within a few miles, the lava cap plateau changed into gentle rolling prairies of knee-high dry grasses. The dog had a lead, and what birds he scared up were too far away for the man to shoot. Red enjoyed watching the bungling mutt pretend he had the skills of a young hunting retriever. Red momentarily forgot about the new world. For, in that moment, he was a young boy watching his first dog work the birds. He was in heaven!

Large cottonwood trees lined a small creek. An accumulation of soft, loamy soil was harbored by the partially exposed roots of a cottonwood at the water's edge. As he passed through, a strong, sticky spider's web struck the brim of his hat. He immediately recognized the texture and strength of the web and tried to stop but couldn't. Red's arms flailed in the air as if he were swatting away a swarm of invisible bees. The dog watched. Red abandoned his hat and shotgun, tossing them to the ground. He danced in tiny quick circles until he was a safe distance away, still frantically rubbing his face and neck with his hands.

The trees were full of spiders' webs, along with their inhabitants. First one, then another and another. The black widows moved with purpose near the ground with their shiny black bodies and red hourglass bellies until they were huddled around their silky white eggs. Large wood spiders with their dusty webs hung high in the limbs and around the trunks of the trees. He shuddered, then surmised, "I'm definitely not in heaven."

He gave the trees a wide berth and continued homeward. Just ahead, a large herd of elk was feeding under the late-afternoon sun. He marveled at the sight like a small boy during his first trip to the zoo.

Red struggled to maintain a hold on the dog. Trying to preserve it for more than a moment was pointless. "Fine, go and show them how tough you are."

Jake sprung out toward the herd. With each leap, Jake would momentarily disappear below the top of the grass. The herd was startled and moved away.

The prairie grass continued for miles, sometimes waist high. Red felt the tips of the grasses tickle the palms of his outstretched hands. There was something next to Red, off to the left. Maybe a single puff of wind or, rather, a low-flying bird. Jake played in the distance, out in front. There it was again. A puff, a whiff of air. A movement traveling through the grass. Red stopped and looked around. Nothing. Nothing except a clear, cloudless blue sky.

He whistled for Jake and clapped his hands together. Jake acknowledged him but didn't obey. Red heard the movement again. Behind him this time. He turned quickly with his gun trained outward. He barely caught sight of a swath of grass tops swaying slightly. There was silence. No thumping of hooves or scurrying of feet. Just the sound of dry blades of grass softly colliding with one another. All was still, and Red stood silent. Jake arrived and bumped into Red's leg. Red gave one last hesitant look around. "OK, boy," he said, but he wasn't really sure.

Four more miles got them to the end of the day. The ground was full of small rodent holes, probably ground squirrels. Red was careful in the placement of his sleeping bag that night. Once comfortably inside the bag, he thought of not only squirrels but of rats and then snakes. He got up, put his boots back on, and stomped down a larger perimeter of the tall dry grass around the campsite. With the heel of his boot, he caved in some of the holes closest to the bag.

The dark night sky overhead was a vast bucket of jewels. He could easily find the Dippers and the W in Cassiopeia in the night sky. He thought of the same sky so many years ago.

"George?" the young voice said quietly in the darkness.

"Yeah?"

"How many stars do ya think are up there?" Red asked.

The two boys lay on their backs. It was warm that night, too warm to be autumn. They'd snuck outside, careful not to wake their sleeping mother. It was a new moon, a perfect night sky to see how many shooting stars they could find.

"Probably billions and billions. See up there, Red, that big square? Most people think that's the Dipper, but it's really Pegasus. And that right there, that's Ursa Minor herself, but people just call her the Little Dipper."

Red thought George was so smart. He seemed to know a little bit about everything. A hoot owl called out nearby, and Red scooted closer to his big brother.

"There ain't nothin' to be afraid of, Red, so get back away from me. It's too hot."

"They're more scared of us than we are of them anyway." George was always right. Calm and reassuring, the stuff big brothers were supposed to be.

"George, are you always gonna be here?"

There was a moment of silence until George whispered, "I'll always be with you, no matter what. Find the North Star."

"Right there."

"Yep. Now from there, go all the way to the east, far as you can, and find the two brightest stars side by side." George waited for Red to find the stars. "Those two stars are the heads of the Gemini twins, Pollux and Castor. See down from their heads, there's their bodies, side by side."

Red concentrated but couldn't find the stars.

"Those lower bright stars going out are their arms, and down from that are their waists, knees, and feet. Connect the dots. Just like stick figures."

"OK, I think I see them now."

"I'll always be here. We'll always have each other, just like Castor and Pollux."

Red was silent.

"All those constellations are all kinda family, related in one way or another. Their momma was Leda, queen of Sparta, their sister was

Helen of Troy. Pollux was born immortal, meaning he could never die. And Castor, he was born mortal, meaning he was more human and could die just like a regular man. They fought in wars and were great horsemen and sailors. But Castor was killed. His brother didn't want to live without him, so he begged his daddy, Zeus, to let him die, too. But Zeus wouldn't have it, so he allowed Pollux to give half of his immortality to Castor. That way, the two brothers lived forever between the gods' world and the real world." Red was trying to understand. "It means we're always gonna be brothers, Red, no matter what."

The two boys pointed skyward, and Red even tried to count the stars. They laughed and told jokes. One passed gas. Then, the gas war was on. They began to tire, and the meadow returned to silence.

"George, why do you and Momma have black hair and I got red?"

"Well, Momma and Daddy found you on the doorstep. They felt sorry for you, so we kept you as our own."

Red quickly sat up. "You mean we ain't really brothers?"

"Well, now, that makes us special brothers, kinda like we picked you. Most people don't have a choice of who they get. Nobody wanted you because of your red hair. That's why I started calling you Red, because I knew other people would tease ya, and I thought you might as well just start gettin' used to it."

"What? Are you kidding me? What's my real name, then?"

George bit his lip and turned his face away from Red.

"Well, let me think. It was so long ago. I think it was something like Hubertus or Francis. Now, don't tell Momma I told you, you'd make her cry for sure."

"But how come we got the same blue eyes, and people say they can't tell us apart yet for the hair?"

"You know, it's kinda like how people end up lookin' like their dogs. You just kind of ended up lookin' like me."

The two boys finally tired and snuck back into their house. It was only a one-bedroom cabin located outside of town. The living room had been made into a makeshift bedroom for the two boys, with their mother sleeping in the only bedroom in the back of the house. The living room was small, with one big sheeted mattress on the floor. The blankets had been thrown to either side of it.

In the darkness, the younger voice whispered, "Why did Daddy leave us?"

George turned away from his brother. "Well, he was just too smart to stay here, and God needed his help." There was silence as George looked out the open window into the darkness. "But he's up there. Right up there in them stars."

"Will you ever leave us?"

"Shoot, if I did, who'd be here to look after ya? I ain't going nowhere. Now shut up and go to sleep."

All was quiet for several minutes. "George? Who's who?"

"What are you talking about?"

Red sat up in bed. "I mean, which one of us is Castor and which one is Pollux?"

Red was startled by the cries of nearby coyotes. Jake was uneasy as well. The fire had gone out and allowed the wilderness to creep in closer. He stoked the fire. The flames were a small, dim light in a world with no boundaries.

CHAPTER 8

In the reddish predawn light, a line of crows flew over the camp and disappeared in the straggly oaks at the base of the hills. The fields teemed with wild game, but Red needed water. He was mad at himself for letting the jugs go empty. It was Jake who found the water first. The dog had gone out of sight near the base of the hills. Red found him lying in a shallow pool of spring water, still panting but definitely pleased with himself. He coaxed the dog out and waited impatiently for the water to clear. Once the canteen and jugs were full, beyond getting home, Red thought of nothing but food.

He stopped near a deep valley he didn't recognize. It'd been the county landfill where the basin had been filled to near capacity. Antelope dotted the grassland, and birds flew above without care. Elk cows and calves chirped like birds, their high-pitched voices contradicting their massive bodies. It was marvelous to witness the bizarre calmness of the wildlife. Surrounded by the simplistic beauty, Red was humbled by its magnificence, in need of nothing. The wildlife did not need his support to live, the winds didn't need his counsel to draft. The grasses were without emotion, the sky without labels, and the trees did not need permission to grow. All were without judgment and asked for nothing in return. They were without mankind.

With the dog at his side, Red soaked in the splendor. "So this is what it looked like. Before we screwed it up." He wished his friends could see this wonder exhibited before him. Then he wished he could see some of his friends—or even some of his enemies.

The northern sky had turned an ominous gray as thunderclouds assembled across the Sierra Nevadas. Red hadn't prepared for rain. The storm was still off in the north, and, hopefully, he would be home before it hit. He looked to the south, out across the valley floor. The Marysville Buttes, forty miles away, severed the valley in half, protruded up through the valley floor, and stood high in the distance with unblemished definition. No longer did a soft purple veil of distant haze conceal the mountains' serrated peaks. Today, he could almost reach out and touch them. Tall rice mills with their cylindrical dryers had once stood on the valley floor encroaching upon the communities of Nelson, Richvale, Biggs, and Gridley. Roads and highways once separated the ranch and farmland into square-like patches of yellows, greens, and browns, forming a tapestry of blended colors in geometrical patterns. Now, there was nothing except a seamless basin of natural creation.

As he was gathering dried wood from a downed tree, a rattlesnake curled up under the brush on a pile of dried cones and rock. It was within striking distance, backed up against the tree trunk. Its tail coiled as the rattles shook in a blur. Red was motionless, already paralyzed as if the snake venom had already taken effect. Jake appeared on the other side of the tree. He barked incessantly at the snake until it retreated and slipped out of sight.

Red had never been afraid of snakes. However, now, in his unforgiving world, things had changed. He moved his camp farther away from the downed tree and added rattlesnakes to his new list of menaces. He would be more vigilant now about the little things like weather changes, blisters, or twisting an ankle. These things were now just as dangerous as the grizzlies and black widows. Red knew he'd die some-day. He would just prefer it to be quick and painless.

Red purposely drank lots of water before going to sleep. He wanted to be sure to wake during the night to relieve himself and, in turn, keep the fire going and the rattler at bay. The dog slept in closer than usual. Red reached out and touched the dog. He stroked Jake's head and shoulders for the first time in recent memory. For some reason, at this point, the dog didn't mind.

The morning brought with it a breeze from the south. After fif-teen miles, it felt good to be back among the pines and dogwoods. He cleared an area under a grove of ponderosas, kicking away the pine cones and making a bed of pine needles for his mattress. The smell of the dried needles and the sound of the wind gently winding its way through the trees were comforting. For a moment, Red felt as if he were just out camping on one of his hunting trips.

For being out of shape, he felt strangely strong and fit. He had done more walking and hiking than he had in years and was neither sore nor achy. His body felt strong. He looked at his hands and stretched out his fingers. The once-swollen joints, misshapen with arthritis, moved freely. He wanted to show Addy, to brag that taking pills had been a waste. He breathed in deeply. No. He wouldn't boast. He'd grab her tightly, hold on, and never let her go.

It was hard to fall asleep. Red could decipher the sounds of most of the woodland creatures, including the distant songs of the coyotes, but there was something different. Something that he couldn't quite make out. He stoked the campfire, returned to his sleeping bag, and fell asleep with his shotgun across his chest.

The wind high above moved the forest into conversation. At night, it was hard to distinguish the wind from approaching danger. A falling limb or twig was quickly interpreted as an intruder's footsteps. Sounds would be magnified, a curious rodent bouncing on the dry leaves of the forest floor transforming into some dangerous, strange, or prehistoric attacking animal.

In the darkness, an oncoming crash busted through the camp. Jake bolted to his feet, barking and snapping. Red belly-crawled to the nearest tree. He wanted to shoot but couldn't tell at what or where.

The campfire only came to life as its disturbed embers were trampled into small bursts of light. First one, then another, and another. The beasts were massive, their weight rumbled through the ground. Red hunkered in a ball. He wanted Jake to do the same. He tried to scream, but nothing came out. He could hear Jake barking from a distance. Jake was alive. The torrent of sound, now slowing. It was over. Over just as abruptly as it had started. Jake's barks turned to growls, then pants as he came closer. "Jake. Jake, come here. Here." Red reached out and pulled Jake in, hugging him. "You OK, huh?"

Nothing but panting, slobbers, and the occasional whimper.

Red swiftly fed the fire. He found his flashlight and scanned around the camp. It was in disarray. The sleeping bag was torn, equipment bashed. The rocks around the fire had been knocked out of alignment and scattered about, the ground littered with forest debris. He crawled on his knees and scrutinized the dirt. "It musta been elk, Jake. Is that what they were?"

Red warily stood up and looked into the darkness, the shotgun held close to his chest. Something had to have been chasing the elk, attacking in the middle of the night, big and deadly.

Red sat guard, flinching with each forest snap, every crunch or change in the wind. Something was hiding, waiting, and Red was its prey. "Jake, come here, boy. Come here next to me."

He tucked Jake in between his knees and held on to his collar with one hand while the other pointed the shotgun into the darkness. He waited for hours, it seemed, Jake long since asleep and curled up in a ball. Red shook the sleep from his head and tended the fire.

A low, rumbling growl came from within the blackness. It wouldn't stop. Red held on to Jake by the scruff of his neck. It was no use telling the dog to shut up—he could barely hang on. The rumble grew louder, turning into an endless wicked scream. The sound didn't come from just one direction. It enveloped the camp, tightly wrapping itself around its potential victim. The barrel of the shotgun pointed to the left, then right, forward and back. His eyes darted side to side searching, penetrating, tunneling into the forest. The scream stopped. The silence was worse. It was hiding, regrouping, lying in wait.

Red let go of Jake, adjusted his grip on the shotgun, and continued to aim into the darkness. The dog barked and snarled without sound. Red could only hear the scream left vibrating in his ears. He felt his rapid breathing and the beating in his chest, but all other senses had shut down. He couldn't think. He needed more light. He kicked more wood into the fire, barely taking his eyes from the muzzle's sights. The growl returned, low and reverberating. Louder and louder, it climaxed in another murderous shriek. A noise no living thing could make. The gun blasted forward, north, then south. Two more shots, each exploding with a ball of light. Then, a click. An empty click. What happened to the gun? Why wouldn't it fire?

Red screamed as he brutally shook the gun in front of him, slamming the palm of his hand into the receiver, again and again. Another empty click. It came to him, flashing through his mind just like that fiery ball of yellow from the shotgun blast. He scrambled to find the box of shells but then remembered he had a handful in his pants pocket. His hands trembled as he reloaded. One in the chamber, one on the ground, then four more in the mag. Jake whined, sniffed in circles, but remained in close.

"It was a mountain lion, Jake. He could've killed you. He could've killed us both." He pulled Jake into his leg and patted him firmly on his neck and shoulder. "You would've been the appetizer." Another fire was built about fifteen feet away from the first. Red sat between the two fires, shotgun across his lap, for the rest of the night. He considered starting a third.

They broke camp at first light and reached the MacNab cypress grove at midday. A black-tailed doe, her fawn, and a yearling stood not fifty feet away. Red was nearly home. He would need fresh meat in the days ahead. He killed the yearling in two shots. The doe and fawn remained close by and watched as the man dressed their fallen.

The additional weight of the meat was taxing over the next several miles. He questioned himself about why he had killed the deer. Rash decision. Surely, he could have killed a buck in his own driveway. Red was tired and wanted to discard the deer meat, but he could not get the image of the two deer watching him butcher the yearling out of his mind. A calmness in their souls, a scene his eyes would not soon erase. How strange this new world and its wild creatures were. Some willing to kill you in the dark of night, and others so unafraid and trusting.

Clouds had formed across the canyon, and the wind freshened from the south. He was glad to finally see the back end of the pickup, the oak tree, and the nearby driveway. He wanted to look up, to see his house, to find it safe. He'd been cast into an irrational nightmare in an unpredictable world. If the house were gone, he'd die without finding his family. He could think of nothing worse.

Pollux and Castor stood silent. As he stepped closer, Red saw the front of the house through the trees. It was there. Nothing had changed. Jake was excited and ran around to the back of the house. For just a moment, Red bore no stress. He was home. He didn't have to hide. He no longer was the hunted. Maybe his old life would magically reappear as he opened the back door. He could sink into the couch with Addy and laugh as he told her his story. She'd kiss him on the face and hug his neck. He opened the back door. "Please, Addy. Be here." The inside of the house was dark. His heart felt the same.

He gathered an armload of dry wood from the woodshed and took it inside as the first drops of rain came down. In short order, the sprinkles turned to a heavy storm. Thunder smashed from every side as lightning lit up the sky, bringing with it a downpour of rain. After two more loads of wood, he rushed inside. Within minutes, the fire began to warm the air and gave light to the inside of the house.

Red put the washtub under one of the outside drain spouts, and in a few hours, it was full. It would be used to water the dog, flush the toilet, and, maybe, bathe in. For the first time, he didn't care about not having electricity. He was happy just to be inside.

He chose a book from Addy's collection and sat next to the fire. It didn't matter what it was about, it just mattered that it was hers, and it was in his hands. *Gifts from the Sea* by Anne Morrow Lindbergh. The book easily fell open to a note card tucked inside. *Mom, for your collection. As I held this book in my hand, I could still remember how you read aloud to us when we were little. Your voice transported me to places only alive in our imaginations. You took me to places that I now have seen as an adult with my very own eyes, places still held deep in my heart. To places you were so happy to be, right along beside me. Thank you for letting me be your son. Happy Mother's Day. Matthew.* He read the first line of the second chapter. Red gently closed the book and returned it to its place. His hand caressed the dark-stained shelf. He felt the wood as if examining it for smoothness. The sounds of hammering and sawing and sanding and laughing came to his mind.

Matthew had managed to talk his high school woodshop teacher into having his class build Addy's library. Extra credit was accrued on the weekends, and more importantly, it got the kids away from the school grounds after fifth period.

"Brilliant, isn't it, Dad," Matthew said quietly as they watched from a corner of the room.

"Mr. Balsdon is quite the teacher. I can't believe this is happening," Red said as he put his arm around Matthew. "Addy's going to be so surprised."

"How much longer do we have before she gets back?"

"We've got one more week."

Matthew took one step forward and shouted, "It looks good, Mr. Bals!"

Mr. Balsdon quickly turned and looked at Matt. He dipped his head, adjusted his glasses, and looked at Red, then back at Matt.

"Sorry, Mr. Balsdon. It looks beautiful!"

Red remembered the sound of the boys' laughter, the smell of freshly cut wood. He smiled and felt the smoothness of the wood and examined the old routing with his finger. He turned and picked up a checkbook from the end table next to Addy's desk. The account balance was $3,800.38. Totally useless. "A bag of gold for a loaf of bread. Is this now my lot?" He carelessly tossed the checkbook on the desk.

Red cleaned and oiled the guns. He was meticulous with them, always had been. Clothing, on the other hand, was carelessly washed in the bathtub with heated rainwater. A bucket to catch the dripping water from the kitchen ceiling would do until the next break in the rain when he would repair the roof. He heated more rainwater and took a bath. The dog was comfortably asleep in front of the fire as the man lay down on his bed with the pistol under the pillow.

The rain stopped. The silence woke Red. He looked at a single star that broke through the clouds, glittering through the raindrops left on the window glass. He asked God for help. But tonight, he felt as if God were as cold and aloof as that distant star. He pulled Addy's pillow into him. It seemed that only just a few days ago, her soft, warm body lay next to him. He remembered the sound of her breathing. He closed his eyes and recalled waking her gently.

CHAPTER 9

The trees had no color, just black outlines, like ink drawings behind the glass. Red lay still and let his soul return, its night-time adventures dimming quickly in his mind. He didn't know how long or even if he had slept at all. But he was glad it was morning.

It was good to wake up inside the house. It felt safe. In that last final moment of sleep, just before consciousness, he knew he was waking up in his own bed, right next to Addy. *Just stay asleep, just one more moment,* he told himself. He slowly opened his eyes, garnering every last second he could possibly steal. There was an indentation on her pillow. She had been there. The house was warm—the woodstove had kept a bed of coals. Last night's teakettle was ready with water for a face wash and a cup of tea. Jake was curled tightly in Addy's overstuffed chair. The dog slowly raised his head toward the man and they exchanged a look of sadness.

"I miss her, too," Red said. "I loved her first, just remember that."

The dog was allowed his stay in the chair as Red sat down on the couch with his cup of tea. He emptied his pants pockets out onto the side table and picked up the small pocketknife. He opened and closed the blade, his eyes unmoving in thought.

Red heard his name being called. George sounded mad and out of breath. Red heard him busting through the woods. He must've been running. George stopped underneath a large oak tree. He was scared. His eyes were alert and scouted all around. He cuffed his hands around his mouth and yelled out for Red. A small limb fell from above and landed on his head. Then another. George looked straight above him and saw his little brother high in the tree.

George took in a deep breath and exhaled from his mouth. For a moment, he looked like he was happy, maybe relieved. His expression soon turned to anger. "Red, what's wrong with you? Haven't you heard me yelling for ya?"

Red took a seat on a long, horizontal overhanging limb, dropped another twig, and said, "Yep."

George shook his head. "Well, why didn't you answer me, then?"

As George climbed up the tree, Red remained silent. George was still out of breath when he sat next to Red on the limb. Both boys' legs hung down over the branch.

"I can see the whole world from here," Red claimed.

George looked around. "Just about."

"But nobody can see me."

"Red, you don't have to run and hide anymore. We're brothers, and we take care of each other."

"I know."

"I'm not gonna let anything happen to us, OK? But you can't hide from me anymore."

Red reluctantly nodded. George handed Red a penny.

Red took the penny and handed it back. "I don't want your stupid measly penny."

"It's more than just a penny. Look here. See right here where it says 'In God We Trust'?"

"Yeah."

"Well, that means that each time you see a penny or even find a penny or pick up a penny, that means God is always with us. It's a reminder to us, every day, that God is here right with us. We're never alone. And knowing that, well, that's worth more than the penny itself." George took out another item from his jeans. It was a small pocketknife. He handed it to Red.

Red looked at the knife but didn't take it. "Momma won't let me carry a knife."

"I'll talk to her about it, OK? Now take it. And besides, I'm not giving it to you, I'm gonna sell it to you."

"Sell it to me?"

"It's bad luck to give a knife away, don't you know that? It'll sever our relationship for sure, and there's no way I'm gonna let that happen. We're bonded forever. We won't ever be severed apart. I just won't let that happen. Now give me that penny, and you just bought yourself a nice pocketknife."

Red quickly paid with the penny and looked closely at the knife. "How do you know that, George?"

"Daddy did the same for me when I was your age. That was his knife, and his daddy most likely did it for him." George looked at the penny as Red held on to his new purchase. George rubbed the face of the coin with his thumb. "'In God We Trust.' He's right here with us, Red. Now let's get out of this tree. With that knife, I don't trust you one bit." George helped Red down. "No more running. No more hiding, OK?"

Lightning flashed, and the sound of its thunder brought Red back. He stood, refilled his cup, and looked around the living room. Bookcases were overfilled with Addy's books, collected over her lifetime. He touched the old floor globe and turned it softly.

The rain outside had been steady for most of the day. George packed and repacked his suitcase several times. Young Red had been teasing his older brother about wearing his slacks and a shirt and tie usually reserved for Sunday church.

"You look like an encyclopedia salesman going door to door."

The laughter stopped.

"Why ya gotta go do this, George?" young Red asked.

"What else you want me to do, Red, stay here while other people fight for our country?" George cleared his throat. "You know, Daddy once told me that I had something special. Something so special that I was gonna share it with the world. But he never quite told me what it was. The only thing I was ever good at, better than anyone else, was hunting and shooting. I can probably already outshoot the best marksman in the whole dang army."

Red turned to hide his face. He was about to lose his best friend. His whole life was changing before his eyes. His emotions were all melded together, and he was afraid he would burst out crying. And boys didn't cry. If he could just marshal the words. "You—you said you'd never leave."

"I ain't leaving, Red, I'll be back right after boot camp. Besides, you know of anyone that can outshoot or out-track your ol' brother?" George grabbed a nearby towel and snapped the end against Red's backside.

Red drank the last sip of warm tea and smiled as he remembered the wrestling match that had followed in the living room of their old house. He wanted to be there again. He remembered telling George goodbye at the bus stop at the edge of town.

George held a dark umbrella. He anxiously glanced down the single-lane road. "OK, here she comes." He looked at his mother, who was standing next to his suitcase. He cocked his head a bit and smiled. "I love ya, Momma."

George wiped the rain from her face and discovered tears. She hugged her son and told him goodbye. The bus stopped, and the door opened in front of them.

George reached out for his brother and said, "I'll be back before you know it."

Red was dying inside. He wanted to tell George how much he loved him and how they should just run away into the mountains forever, but he could not open his mouth. George hugged him and wouldn't let go.

Red fought back tears, then feigned a look of disgust. "Let go of me, people are gonna think you're a queer or something."

Both smiled and then laughed as they batted one another away. George picked up his suitcase, got on the bus, and walked down the aisle. Red walked parallel down the sidewalk and stopped at the bus window where George was sitting down.

"Hey, Georgie, don't be kissing any of those boys now." Red laughed.

The bus lunged forward, and George stuck his head out the window and yelled, "When I get back, remind me to kick your butt."

The bus drove out of sight with both boys still waving at one another.

Red stopped the globe from spinning. He was alone again, unable to share, incapable of feeling another's touch. Loneliness was different than solitude. Loneliness was deep, dark, and utterly empty. A place where pain remained—somewhere he didn't want to be.

He spent the day going over and gathering things he would need for his next search. Winter was coming fast, and he would use the house for base camp during the worst of the weather. He carried his pistol and extra ammo around his waist. He wanted to pretend he was safe in his own backyard, but the wariness never left. He couldn't explain it. Something was there, watching him. Waiting.

He stacked firewood next to the house under the back porch so it'd be easier to retrieve when the snow hit. It would be his only source of heat, and nature had provided plenty of wood. He looked at the piled-high stack, enough to last a season. He didn't plan after that. He would find his Addy, his family, and his life again.

His mind went back and forth between preparing for winter and seeking answers. His search trips would be short but cover all directions, as far out as he could go. Red busied himself throughout the day. He built a tripod from iron T-posts to sit over Dante and hung a pot of stew over the fire. He took his shotgun, a five-gallon bucket, and Jake down to the old oak tree. He spent the better part of the morning picking up acorns from beneath the oak. Years back, Red had made acorn mush for breakfast, which he ate with feigned enthusiasm in front of Matthew and Sam. He closed his eyes and thought he could hear their laughter. They must've been ten or twelve then. The taste of the raw acorn meat was just as tannic as eating a raw olive from the tree, or maybe a green persimmon. He hammered the meats into smaller pieces and put them in a pan of cold water to leach overnight.

The living room was finally warm, a pot of tea steaming on top of the woodstove. Red studied Addy's chair as he gently sat down. He touched the leather arm, just about where her hand would rest. If only he could hold her hand, he'd never let go. The dog watched from across the room. Jake didn't move, even when politely called.

"Did I ever tell you about the first time I saw her? She was beautiful. Oh, don't get me wrong. I was never one for all that glamour and make-up stuff, but, I mean, she was beautiful from the inside out. Prettier than any movie star ever could be." Red smiled at the thought. He felt the warmth returning to his soul, the yearning back into his heart. "I fell in love with her the first time I set eyes on her. I loved everything about her. I watched her from a distance. I couldn't take my eyes off her. The way she spoke with people. How she held little Sam's hand."

Red paused, lowered his head, and smiled.

"Sam. She grew up to be just as beautiful as her mother, didn't she? Just with a bit more attitude, though. You'd know all about that."

Jake raised his head.

Red sighed and leaned back in the chair. "I wanted to ask her to marry me right then and there. I imagined walking over to her and taking her hand in mine, just to see if she was real. She woulda thought I was crazy. Probably called the cops on me."

Hearing the words aloud made him feel warm and safe, but only until the silence stole them back, leaving sorrow and isolation in their place. Red finished his tea and went back outside. Jake waited for the man to leave the room before he climbed up in Addy's chair, curled into a ball, and went to sleep.

Red spent most of the afternoon picking the apples from Addy's small orchard: three trees, a Red Delicious, a Honeycrisp, and a McIntosh, all surrounded by a tall wire fence. He shooed the deer away more than once. They acted like he was the intruder who refused to leave their territory. He stood nearly on the top step of the ladder, making one last reach upward.

It became eerily calm. The birds stopped singing, the frogs ceased croaking, the forest became completely still, and the deer had silently disappeared without notice. Red quietly stepped from the ladder and removed his pistol from his belt. Jake was gone. The screen door screeched open as Red shuffled backward into the house. He scrutinized the edge of the forest. "Jake, here, boy. Come on, here, boy." A little louder this time: "Jake?"

A startling knock came from behind him, inside the house. He quickly turned, gun in hand. It was Jake, his tail wagging and hitting the kitchen cabinet. Red slammed and locked the door. He leaned his back against the inside of the door, tossing the bag of apples onto the table. It was getting to him. He was no longer someone who relished adventure or craved excitement. He was a mouse. A little brown mouse cowering in a corner, not sure which way to turn. Rational thoughts were becoming fewer and fewer, and he knew it.

Normal sights and sounds were transposed into abnormal concepts. It was his onset of old age. Dementia. He had lost his mind and was living in his own world. His imagination had pulled every cogent thought from his brain and replaced them with those of a madman. This was what it felt like to be crazy. Addy was right there next to him taking care of his daily needs. He was a prisoner in his own mind. Locked up somewhere in unwashed clothes with the sour smell of old age. No, Addy would not allow that. She was taking care of him, feeding and bathing him.

"Addy. Can you hear me, honey? I'm right here in front of you. I'm right here. Tell me what to do, just tell me what to do. I want to come back to you. Addy!" His chest muscles were in a fierce battle, refusing to let in air. He slid to the floor and collapsed.

The last flicker of light spilled out into the darkness, bringing with it memories of his wife and family, along with vulnerabilities, fear, and the reality of death. Life, a delicate and precious gift. It had been snatched away without notice or cause.

CHAPTER 10

Sometime during the night, Red had moved to the couch. He was jarred awake by the sound of an elk bugling outside, merged with Jake's shrill barking inside. He'd heard that sound before, in Montana and once in Colorado. He dashed to the closest window. The massive cow had annihilated the apple trees and was standing among what was left of them and eating what was probably the last apple. In his excitement, he called out to Addy, "Come look at this, honey! Quick!" He thought "Buttercup" would be a perfect name for the cow. She was beautiful! Maybe "Eleanor." *Eleanor the Elk!*

A shroud of wretched coldness overpowered him. His gut was heavy, pulling down, sagging his shoulders with the realization he was in a life he didn't want. Addy wasn't there. Whether he was delusional or somehow thrust into another dimension, he'd have to fight until he found his way home.

"Jake. Shut up. You can't go out yet." Red had to be careful. The elk could be dangerous. They were interlopers from a different time. That was an odd thought; it'd never occurred to him before. Danger. Danger versus fear—the difference, that is. Danger was tangible, solid, and real. But fear? Fear was created, a product of his mind. Like a gas, able to pass through things effortlessly. It overtook and invaded coherent thoughts and infected them like a cancer. Was able to suffocate and destroy from the inside out, leaving a body with no skeletal support. That was what would kill him. Fear!

The elk wandered into the woods. Jake bolted out as Red guardedly opened the door. A layer of fog had set in overnight. For a moment, Jake disappeared into the mist, but Red could still hear him walking about. Red gave him a few more moments, then called out, "Jake, come on, Jake. Get back in here." Nothing, no dog, no sounds. "Jake! Now!"

Red slowly walked into the silent fog. *How could a dog disappear so quickly? Why did I even let him out?* The fog consumed all sense of direction and twisted landmarks into unfamiliar and hostile sites. He was instantaneously vulnerable. Within fifty feet of his own back door, Red was adrift in the middle of a foggy sea without his bearings. Something was running. Running fast and directly at him. Red managed to react quickly enough to move the rifle out in front. His death would be swift and close, and probably over in seconds. He wanted to shoot into the fog, jump-start his chance of survival.

Jake vaulted through the fog, wagging his tail, and circled around Red. Fear left Red's body just as fast as it had intruded. He felt his stomach turn, bile already rising to his mouth. It was worse than almost falling and catching yourself just before you hit the ground. Sometimes taking the fall was easier than the save. He leaned forward and tasted the thick wetness in his mouth, fear's residual effect.

"Let's go home, boy. Let's get some chow, OK, chow!"

"Chow," the word that would prompt Jake to take the most direct route to the back door. Red closely followed.

It was good to see, smell, and taste fruit again. He could eat every apple he'd picked within days but thought he might ration them the best he could. Red gathered the apples from the kitchen table and those that had fallen to the floor. He held a large apple up to his face and breathed in the aroma. Addy's voice was clear. "It smells of Vermont!" He thought about a time long ago. It was a Saturday morning, and he found Addy in the backyard digging three large holes.

"Addy, what are you doing?"

Addy wiped the sweat from her brow and took a deep breath. "Well, since you won't take me to Vermont, I'm bringing Vermont to us."

"You're planting maple trees for syrup?"

"No, but that's a good idea. Apples! Three varieties." Addy pushed the shovel back into the damp ground.

"The deer will annihilate them."

"That's where you come in, dear. You're charged with building a deer-proof fence. Now go get your shoes on."

"Who's gonna take care of them? Prune them, and they need to be sprayed two or three times a year. Then who's gonna pick them? We don't have an orchard ladder."

"Again, that's where you come in."

Red thought about the times Addy had spoken about Vermont. He knew it had been a special place for her. She had spent summers there with her grandmother as a kid while her parents were away in New York. They'd picked apples each autumn from Massie's Orchard. She had talked about it so intimately, he felt like he had actually been there. Cider jelly, pure maple syrup, and fat white sheep dotting the deep-green hillsides. Her family had maintained a summer home near Cabot Pond up until her father died years back. Red always seemed to have some type of convenient excuse not to visit the area with her. Now, it would be the first place he would take her.

He retrieved a pair of nylon pantyhose from Addy's dresser. She kept them in the top drawer, along with her scarves and handkerchiefs. He slid a silk scarf through his fingers, once a simple, insignificant act, now so reverent and meaningful. It was her favorite, the yellow one. He drew the scarf to his face and breathed in Addy. The smell of lingering perfume inebriated his senses. It was all he had left of her. "I'll come back to you, honey, I promise you that."

Red took the bounty of apples under the house. The parcel was sloped and allowed one end of the home to have an area underneath it almost the size of a small basement. It had a dirt floor but was pretty much rodentproof. It was cool and dry and would serve as his cellar. He hung the pantyhose from the floor joists and filled them with apples.

He spent the better part of the day crushing the acorn meat and setting it to boil until it was the consistency of Cream of Wheat. Even with added salt and fresh apples, it was terrible. Time to try something else. The fog had lifted somewhat, but the fear of it returning kept Red within sight of the house. Red retrieved his shotgun and a canvas sack and took the dog down the gravel driveway. He looked for two of the foods he knew had grown in the forests nearby, rose hips and tree mushrooms. He'd forgotten about wild onions until he saw Jake peeing on a clump near where the mailboxes used to be. "Well, Jake, I guess we won't get any more junk mail." Red smiled. "And no more bills."

The sounds of wilderness were all around. Birds chirped high above while squirrels chased one another up, around, and upside down in the pine trees. Red filled his backpack with supplies to last several days. It was a little heavier this time, but he felt strong and capable. He would go east, toward Matthew's house, then to Sam's. She lived south from there. East was drier country. It meant fewer streams, more exposure to sun, and, subsequently, fewer greens and berries to eat. The thoughts reminded him to eat.

Red left his backpack on the table, picked up his shotgun, and slung it over his shoulder. "Come on, hound dog, let's go get some veggies for the trip." *Blackberries, wild grapes, mushrooms, onions, and water lettuce!* He was like a small boy scouting the forest floor, searching for provisions on a Boy Scout instructional camping trip.

The blackberry bushes were as tall as trucks. The berries were dry and had withered into small raisin-like morsels. He plucked the dried berries one by one but searched deeper into the patch for a juicier prize. He wondered why he had not scared up any quail or grouse in the patch. Something was odd. Red froze. The silence was uncanny. He looked left, then right. A great black bear rose from the bush. The bear stood on its hind feet and roared with force.

They were face to face, man to beast. The only thing Red could see in the entire world was the bear's wet snarl. Thick saliva dripped out. The teeth were yellowed, and the smell was horrific. The roar lasted forever. He could've reached out and touched the beast had he been able to move. He couldn't move to get the shotgun hanging on his shoulder. He wanted his feet to run but felt them still flat on the ground. He needed to gasp for air, but his lungs had closed tightly. Adrenaline screamed at him to run. He wanted to faint but couldn't even do that. How gruesome his death would be. He would never find Sam or Matt, and Addy would be lost forever.

The front of his khaki trousers darkened with wetness. The bear turned and charged toward Jake. Red was deaf. He saw the dog snarling and lunging toward the bear but heard no sounds. Jake darted back and forth, retreated, then charged again. The fight created an upheaval of dirt, and Jake was shrouded in a cloud of dust. Red saw his arm pull the shotgun sling from his shoulder. His arms held the gun out in front of him. He felt the trigger pull. The butt slammed into his shoulder, but he heard nothing. The gun must've gone off.

The bear fell to the ground, landing solidly in the berry bushes. Red continued to shoot, but there was no sound. There must be something wrong with the gun. He fired more rounds and reloaded with fresh shells. He fired again. He saw the empty casings on the ground as he stepped backward and wondered how they all got there. He shouted for Jake. He barely heard his own voice but felt the vibrations in his throat. There it was, so low it could barely be heard. "Jake! Get back, Jake!" And again, a little louder, "Jake!"

He was no longer the confident hunter of his youth. His once-staunch pride depleted, no longer allowing him to walk on water. Now, he was only an expendable man at the mercy of nature. Red had to sit down for a while. He didn't know how long he sat next to the dead bear before his mind was clear. His heart resumed beating at a normal pace, and his hearing apparently returned. Jake paced back and forth and appeared proud to have been a part of the adventure. Red had survived. It had been the closest to death he'd ever been. He'd fought, and he'd won. It was a beast, but he was stronger and smarter.

Red touched the bear and was surprised at the coarseness of the hair. His hand was still shaking, but he didn't try to hide it. Not that he was embarrassed but rather because it didn't matter anymore. The bear's face was gone, shot away several times. Its large hind feet protruded from the berry vines. Had there not been so much blood, it would have looked like the bear was asleep on his back. Red glanced over at Jake. His voice quivered as he said, "That'll teach him to take our jerky."

across the vault of heaven. Red vowed to never camp on a mountaintop again. Both dog and man slept for the remainder of the night.

It seemed morning came as soon as Red fell asleep. Not far down the ridge, his nighttime vow took on new importance. He passed a huge old pine tree that had been hit by lightning. It was blown to pieces, with big chunks of wood scattered across a fifty-yard circle. One large, long piece stood stuck in the earth thirty yards from the tree. It looked like a huge lance thrown down by Zeus himself. The lower portion of the tree still stood, but it was now a collection of long planks that had been split apart by the strike and were only held together by the stump. The smell of fresh pinewood reminded him of when he'd passed by newly cut timber at the local mill when he was a boy. He thought of his brother.

Red sat outside the perimeter fence of the lumber company, waiting for his brother to get off work from his summer job. Red looked down the driveway leading into the mill. Nothing. He threw three more rocks at a fence post, hitting it only once. Another look down the road. A truck drove out, but it wouldn't be George. He'd be walking. The late afternoon still harbored the summer's heat. Red looked for shade and found a spot under a fir where he could still see the front gates of the mill. Finally, George walked out and Red bounced to his feet.

"C'mon, we only gotta couple more hours of daylight," Red pleaded.

George, obviously tired and hot, smiled and picked up the pace and halfway jogged toward his little brother. Red was wearing just his overalls and shoes, while George had on a short-sleeved shirt, trousers, and leather work shoes, all covered with sawdust and sweat.

"All right, all right, I'm here," he said.

The brothers walked side by side down a dirt lane bordered on each side by overgrown blackberry vines covered with a thick layer of dust from the road. It didn't really matter to Red what they were doing or where they were going. It only mattered that they were together.

"I saw six or seven hens and toms on the way here down at the old apple orchard. Do you think by the time we walk home and get the shotgun, they'll still be there?" Red asked.

"Pretty sure—they don't seem to move too fast. Maybe afterward we can go swimming in the river."

The boys reached their house. George quietly unlocked a padlock on a cabinet in the kitchen. He reached in and removed a double-barreled shotgun and a .22 rifle and cautiously made sure each was unloaded. He gave Red a handful of shells to put into his overall pockets. George handed the opened shotgun to Red. He knew the drill. Unloaded, barrel to the ground, at least until out of sight of the house. George was careful to relock the cabinet, checking it twice.

As the boys walked down the road and crossed over into the woods, Red asked, "George, why is Momma so afraid of guns?"

George grunted, curled his lip, and shrugged one shoulder.

"She always gets so scared when she sees us going hunting or shooting at targets. It's like she doesn't like to see or hear them."

"Some people are just like that, I suppose. She likes it when we bring home stuff to eat, and she likes making us jerky and stews, but she just doesn't like to see the guns. That's why we gotta be real careful. We gotta make sure they're always clean, unloaded, and locked away. She doesn't mind us using them, just not around her."

Red was quiet. He looked at the grain in the wood stock and followed the pattern with his fingers. "We gotta respect how Momma feels, even though we don't feel that way, because that's the right thing to do."

George nodded.

By the time the boys got to the abandoned orchard, there was no sign of the turkeys. Red and George looked for grouse, squirrels, or anything that might be suitable to eat, but they found nothing. Red wanted to shoot an old cranky crow circling above. It landed in a treetop and scared up several blackbirds and a noisy blue jay. Red sighted in on the jay.

"Don't be shooting anything we can't eat, Red, you know that."

The hunt had been unsuccessful. Both boys ambled down the dirt road and headed for home. "George, you ever eat a blue jay?"

"No."

"Then how do you know they can't be eaten?"

"Red, don't be such a moron. You can't eat blue jays, and you can't shoot them."

Red talked George into having a shooting contest with the BB gun in the backyard. Their mother didn't mind the BB gun as much as the rifles, as long as the boys didn't get out of hand. They set up empty tin cans, and the challenge began. The yard was unfenced, and it bordered a wooded area on the back side and overgrown empty lots on either side. Competition was fierce. George never allowed Red to win simply. Rather, Red had to earn it. The tiebreaker involved a tin can tied to a string and hung from a tree limb at the edge of the woods. George swung the can. A new rule was enacted after Red waited for it to nearly stop, then hit the can dead center: you must shoot within five seconds. Even with the new sanction, Red was coming in ahead. George was about to make the deciding shot. A large tom turkey and its harem sauntered into the backyard. It was a huge turkey. Red was beside himself.

"George," Red whispered, "would you look at him? It's like he wants us to shoot him, he wants us to have him for dinner."

"I know, he'd be so easy to take, and we do need meat right now. He would make a fine stew." George looked around briefly, laid the BB gun on the ground and picked up his .22 rifle. He checked the chamber and held it out to his little brother. Red reached for the gun. He looked up at his brother as if asking for permission. "Go ahead, just be real careful. And be quick about it."

It's what Red had waited for all day. From the time he'd left the house in the early morning, then waiting for George most of the day, it was all he could think about. The tom was huge, with puffed feathers flared into a vertical fan. It would be the grand prize at the end of a long, long day. Red's steady aim masked his excited insides. He took careful aim and slowly pulled the trigger.

Before Red could lift his eyes from the sights, he heard his mother scream George's name. The bird dropped as George and Red turned to the back door of the house. The windows were open. The summer breeze made the kitchen curtains flutter inside. Red's mother ran from the house through the back door. She was still in her work clothes. Her white hospital smock, still clean, starched, and orderly, was in stark contrast to the woman beneath it. She was a person of uncommon gifts. Things that were difficult for others came easily to her. She calmed the most challenging of patients with just her presence. Their worrying thoughts were eased, and their anxious questions were answered with wisdom and unpretentious concern. With just a touch, she could turn the fear in her patients' eyes into looks of trust and respect. But now, it was her eyes that were filled with terror, her face devoid of color. Her emotional pain came bursting out.

"George, George! What happened!" she screamed as she ran toward Red.

Again and again, George said he was sorry. "I didn't know you were home, Momma. It's all right, it's just a turkey for dinner. It's OK. It's OK. We're OK. Nothing happened, Momma. It was just a turkey. It's all my fault. We're all right."

Red's mother was inconsolable. Tears fell freely as her arms clamped around each boy. Beyond all natural means of soothing, she cried in such a desolate way, her sobs only interrupted by her need to breathe.

Red didn't say a word as he was tugged in tightly. Never before had he seen his mother so terrified. It didn't make sense. Neither Red nor George had been careless, and the shot had not been reckless, but her reaction said otherwise. He'd committed a heinous crime but didn't know what it was. Red held on to his mother. He didn't know what else to do. Her chin quivered, like she was the child.

CHAPTER 21

The country was rugged, with tall, rocky cliffs and low, dense brush surrounded by thick forests of evergreens. The alpine meadows near the top of the mountains made the going easier. Fool hens were everywhere, as were signs of deer, elk, and at least one grizzly. There was no mistaking it: based on the size and depth of the paw prints in a patch of snow, it was an enormous bear.

"So much for hibernation."

Red was nearing Lake Almanor. He'd make an early camp there and try to smoke the leftover sheep meat during the light of day. It would be easy at night to do so while he slept, but it was probably not the smartest way to keep midnight looters away.

Red had been eating rose hips from his pack supply since leaving home. He was somewhat familiar with edible plants, collecting various greens along the way. He found a supply of chokecherries and chick-weed mixed in with some mountain sorrel. He wanted to keep a good supply of the rose hips for further on in the trip when fresh greens might not be available. Red knew he was burning more calories than he was taking in. He also needed fat. Specifically, bear fat, the most nutritious he could eat. However, killing and harvesting a bear would have to wait until he arrived at his winter home. It'd be there that he could salvage most of the meat and save the hide. With that thought, he decided to start with a cup of hot spruce tea.

The camp was cleaned and packed by the time the sun rose over the eastern mountains. Red was full of energy and felt a bit of excitement about reaching his winter goal. It was a plan, a direction. He was taking action, now focused on the goal of finding the cave near Denver. Come springtime, he and Jake would start out across the country once again.

He walked at least six miles before reaching a big meadow near Deer Creek. He'd made good time. He was tired. His legs hurt, and his shoulders and hips ached badly from carrying the pack. The area was covered in meadow grass, relatively flat, and not too far from the creek. Deer Creek was clear, cold, and full of big trout finning at the end of every ripple.

The tree trunks were scarred with fresh beaver markings. Red had eaten beaver only once as a young man. He recalled reading about old-time fur trappers not only taking their hides but also using their abundant fat for cooking. He could use the fat, but he told himself to be smart with his time. If he didn't get to Denver, to his cave, winter would kill him.

After camp was set up, Red took his compact fishing rod and returned to the creek. In short order, he caught three big rainbow trout, which he filleted and cooked over the open fire along with the rest of the sheep meat.

The fillets were tender, some falling off the stick and into the fire. Jake preferred the sheep meat, and Red would rather have fried the fish. He thought about the acorn flour in his pack. He needed grease, salt and pepper, and dill. Yes, fresh dill, and lots of it. After dinner, he studied his maps, made entries, and drew lines along the shortest routes and the easier courses. He fell asleep thinking about fried fish.

The fire was just a pile of ashes by morning. He raked out a coal and, with a few dry pinecones, started it again. The morning was cool, and the fire felt good. A bald eagle screeched overhead. Its wings spread out, resembling a cross, then it disappeared to the east. A party of stellar jays hung around, calling from tree to tree. "What are you guys trying to tell me? The secret code? I'm doing good?" Red smiled. The familiar bird sounds made it seem like he was back home again. All he needed was a hot cup of coffee with cream, a buttered bagel, and the morning paper. And maybe some bacon and eggs.

The North Fork of the Feather River ran fast and cold. The river was about forty yards wide. A small gravel bar split the river down the middle. The first section of water was shallow and fast. The second appeared deep but swift. Several hundred yards down, on the opposite side, was a gravel bar. Red could walk across the first section, but on the second section, he'd have to swim downstream to get across to the bar. The problem would be Jake. Jake wasn't a strong swimmer, but he'd always loved the water and showed no fear.

Over the last several months, Jake had become stronger than Red ever remembered him to be. In the past, Red had never really been concerned about the dog. He loved all animals, took care of them, provided for them, and made sure they remained healthy. But with Jake, it had been similar to owning an outdoor barn cat to keep mice and squirrel out of the hay bales. Just when Red would let his guard down and accept him, Jake would growl or snip. Just like a barn cat. Red watched Jake play in the shallow water, barking and bouncing as if inviting Red to come in as well. Red felt he had lost everything he had ever loved except for one large, overzealous, temperamental dog.

Jake took one large leap into the river and crossed over the shallow rapids to the bar, splashing and thrashing. "A great leap of faith, my friend." Red inflated the inner tube with the small hand pump, took off all his clothes, and put on his tennis shoes. He placed the entire pack, along with the dog's nylon saddlebag, into a large, thick plastic duffel bag, sealed it, and tied it to the inner tube. He secured his guns to the top of the pack, leaving the shotgun loose enough that he could remove it in a hurry. He put his holster around his shoulder and torso like it was a bandolier and pushed the platform into the water. The water was knee deep. He stumbled a couple of times because of the fast current but made it to the gravel bar where Jake waited for him.

The next leg would be risky. He'd have to go first and pray that Jake would follow. The dog would have to swim hard to get across. He thought about putting Jake on top of the raft, but it already was too top heavy. Another hundred pounds of moving weight would surely capsize it. Tying a rope to Jake could prove to be fatal if the current swept either one away. The only chance to make it would be by floating downstream rather than just swimming straight across. If he lost his pack and guns, he'd likely die. If he lost his dog, his only companion, he would definitely die.

Red played a game with Jake in an attempt to get the dog excited enough to follow him into the water. Red pushed the platform into the river in front of him while he held on to the back end. The water was cold and deep. He kicked his legs and called out to Jake. The dog reluctantly jumped in and began to follow. Jake fought the current. Jake's head stuck out of the water with his hind end low beneath the surface. The current turned Jake around. He struggled to keep aimed toward the shore as his front legs slapped up and down, in and out of the water.

The man made landfall as the dog continued down the river close to the shore. Red was quick to his feet. He made sure his raft was on the bar before he chased after the dog. Red called out, "Jake! Come on, Jake!" A bend in the river concealed its course. Red ran as fast as he could. His mind fabricated scenes of Class IV rapids and white waterfalls cascading over cliffs. He could feel his mind panicking.

About eighty yards downstream, Jake was able to reach the riverbank but went out of sight in the tangle of vegetation. Red dropped to his knees in either exhaustion or relief, or maybe both. Jake was safe, or, at least, out of the water. Red had left his shotgun back on the gravel bar with the pack. Now, the man was naked, alone, and frightened.

Jake came bounding out through the wild grapes and berry bushes. Red never recalled seeing Jake so playful. He waited for Jake to shake, pee, and shake again.

"You're quite the lard ass, aren't you," the man said as he hugged the dog. "We're gonna have to work on your style and technique next time."

Red returned to the pack, got dressed, and hugged his wet, stinky dog again.

The river was clear and odorless, with bits of chewed green branches littering the edge along with discarded clamshells—evidence of beaver and river otters. A few salmon rolled every now and then. That was maybe to Red's good fortune: fewer salmon, fewer bears. He rechecked his gear and supplies, deflated the inner tube, and meticulously repacked his backpack.

Red felt relieved. Crossing the river had been chancy. *But we did it, damn it.* He thought he heard his wife's voice reciting one of her familiar expressions: "Never trouble trouble till trouble troubles you." Addy was back, next to him.

He smiled. He had his own theory about trouble. He looked down at Jake. "You know, the trouble with trouble is that it always seems to start out as fun." For a moment, Red returned to his childhood.

The river water was cool and offered relief from the summer's heat. The water reflected the greenness of the assortment of cottonwood trees and vines. George dunked Red under the water, and, in turn, Red blasted George with a full splash to the face. Cattle were nearby, and Red could see at least one heifer farther down the sluggish river. She was belly deep, standing near the shore. She must've been standing in the water for some time, as the surface was still and her reflection was near perfect.

"Come on, Red, we better head back."

The two boys got dressed and headed home. As they walked down the dirt road, the wetness of their underwear dampened their jeans. But it didn't matter.

"Let's cut through the pasture," Red said as he grabbed on to the barbed-wire fence.

George pulled the top wire up and made enough space for Red to pass through without being scratched. Once he was through, Red put his foot on the bottom wire and held it down as his brother crawled through the opening.

The pasture was thick, green, and humid from the summer irrigation. The cattle were assorted Angus, Herefords, and various half-breeds. George slowed his pace as he looked ahead. "What's that?"

Red perked up and tried to see.

Farther ahead, there was some type of motion in the deep pasture grass. As they approached, the boys scared off a small fawn that took refuge near a wild blackberry patch on the fence line. George and Red hurriedly walked closer to the commotion. It was a doe, tangled in the barbed-wire fence. She was cut and bleeding. She flailed her legs and kicked to get away from the humans. George stopped and pulled back on Red.

"She's all caught up," George said.

The doe kicked and wiggled. It was useless, though. She was trapped.

"Let's get her out!" Red demanded.

"No, we can't get any closer, or she'll kick us with her hooves."

Red looked at the fawn. Her white spots were still visible, and her long mule ears fluttered with concern.

"We got to get her out, or she'll die."

George looked at the fawn and then back to its mother. "She's really caught up in there, Red. If I had my rifle, I'd put her out of her misery right now."

"No, we can get her out."

"Even if we could, she would end up dying. Look at those cuts."

Red pulled away from his brother as if about ready to throw a punch at him. "No, George, the blood makes it look worse than it is. They're only as deep as the barbs. She has a baby, and it's gonna die without her."

George paused and thought. "OK, OK, we gotta be careful, though. If I say 'let go,' you better damn well let go, do you hear me?" Red rarely heard his brother cuss. The situation was serious. He had heard George use "dang," "dag nabbit," "Jesus," and "hell." But "damn" was usually reserved for those occasions when someone was about to get walloped.

The doe kicked and thrashed as much as she could. George held on to the barbed wire until she tired, settled down, or gave up. George took off his belt and looped it over the two top strands of barbed wire, then pulled and latched them together. He took off his shirt and told

Red to do the same. George tore Red's shirt in half and wrapped one half around one of the center strands and told Red to hold on to it for dear life as he wrapped the other half around his left hand.

George placed his shirt close to the doe near two of her tangled legs. "Put your foot right on that bottom wire, and whatever you do, don't let it up."

Red put his foot on the strand. He pushed down slowly until the wire was firm against the ground.

George pulled and pried and yelled out to Red to hold on and pulled some more. The doe writhed and snorted. Finally, she was free. The deer bolted out, half surprised or maybe in shock. George and Red watched her bounce like a rabbit as she reunited with her baby. Her tail flitted with what must've been appreciation.

George put his hands on Red's shoulders, and the shirtless boys smiled as they watched mother and baby hop off into the distance.

"You did good, Red, you did good."

Red grinned and straightened his shoulders. George was proud of him.

George wiped the deer's blood from his hands and face. As they turned for home, Red handed George his shirt back. George gave Red his half shirt and said, "Except now you've got to explain to Momma how your shirt got ripped in half."

CHAPTER 22

For the next several miles, the area was covered with large meadows with the occasional burst of alder trees. There were lots of Canada honkers flying overhead, always to the east. "I'm coming, Addy."

A beaver had dammed a small creek, which flooded a portion of the north side of the meadow. Every pond was full of ducks, mostly cinnamon teal and mallards. Every corner fostered life, from eagles and osprey with nests high in the perimeter trees to great blue herons and even an occasional seagull. "Look, Jake, there's my old friend Jonathan Livingston."

He'd made good time over the last week and talked himself into hunting beaver for the meat and fat. He couldn't take for granted that food would always be available. The fat would keep and provide the nutrients he would need.

The pond was home to a pair of mallard ducks. He sat at the base of the tree and held his pistol in his hand. The dog apparently needed rest, as well, and slept at the man's side until a shot from the pistol startled him back to his feet.

The beaver was near the middle of the pond. Red hadn't planned well for the recovery. He quickly stripped down to his underwear and waded into the water. The pond was deep and cold. The beaver must've weighed fifty pounds. The hide was thick and beautiful, but Red knew time would not allow him to render it into a pelt. He took the hindquarters, tail, and all the fat from beneath the hide.

Red fried up the remaining fish fillets after dusting them in acorn and root flour. It was a welcome change. He reduced the remaining beaver fat well into the night, being careful to recover any liquid grease. He hung the remaining fresh beaver meat high in a tree, several feet from the camp.

He watched a coyote try and sneak up on a goose family and fail miserably. He knew coyotes were a menace. Notorious for their troublemaking, killing farm animals and anything vulnerable in nature, he generally thought they should be shot on sight. But now, for some reason, he felt sorry for the creatures. They weren't attractive animals, really. Sometimes, if you looked at them just right, most resembled underfed, neglected dogs. But that was part of their charm.

Coyotes and a horned owl sang their nighttime songs while bullbats flew overhead, making disconcerting roaring noises as they chased bugs near the firelight. Lightning flashed far off in the distance toward the west at least twenty or thirty miles away. Its delayed thunder made a low, haunting rumble. The man brought the dog in close, and both fell asleep.

He kept his bearing headed east. If the weather held, today would be his bath and laundry day. He could still smell the grease in his beard and on his hands and shirt. At midday, he startled a herd of elk that had been drinking from a creek. As the herd crashed off, Red realized he had been lost in thought. Memories of his childhood. His brother had been so real, so comforting. Memories he hadn't thought of in years. He had inadvertently allowed himself to lose his sense of orientation. Adrenaline flooded through his bloodstream. A quick look at the compass in his walking stick confirmed his eastbound travel. But that wasn't enough. He pulled the bigger compass from his shirt. Yes. Eastbound. How quickly he became uncertain and anxious surprised him. He rubbed his face and head with his hand and decided as soon as the hair on his head lay flat again, he'd cut it off and bathe.

He trimmed his hair and beard as close as he could with the scissors without cutting himself. He cleaned his teeth, flossed with fishing line, and clipped his nails. He'd brought a small, half-used bar of soap that he used sparingly to wash his face and hands. His feet were sore and cramped. The pot of water was near boiling. He poured a cup of tea, manzanita berries steeped in water, and pretended it was good. He soaked a dirty T-shirt in the rest of the hot water, then wrapped his bare feet with the steaming wet shirt. Had the pot been big enough, he would've submerged his entire body.

The nighttime silence was disturbing. The air was empty of white noise and ambient light. Red strained to pick up any noise other than the fire and an owl somewhere behind him. He wished he could trade places with the bird, as his mind pictured the monsters just outside the firelight as massive beasts, almost invincible: huge heads lifted, noses wrinkling, little pig eyes watching with intense purpose.

The morning replaced the man's fear with gratitude. He had gone through this area many times in the past. He was overwhelmed with memories. He remembered a Saturday afternoon football championship his young son participating in, having a nice dinner at the Pioneer Café, and staying overnight in a motel with his beautiful wife. He remembered being in a hunting accident in the nearby area many years ago. He had almost died. Addy had been there when he'd woken up in the hospital. The memories sapped him of energy.

The pain was unbearable. The gurney bumped into the curb after being unloaded from the ambulance. Red screamed in pain and couldn't understand why someone was asking him who was president and for his date of birth when he was about to die.

"I'm fifty-two." He winced in pain.

He heard footsteps running toward him. It was Addy. He recognized the sound immediately. Red felt himself calm. She was there now, and everything would be all right. She was in her work clothes, spotless and sharp. Addy grabbed on to the side of the gurney, followed it inside the hospital, and made sure Red knew she was there. Their eyes met, and her voice trembled when she tried to speak. She cleared her throat and started again. "I'm right here, Red. I'm not going to leave you."

Red was unshaven, dirty, and sweaty. His white T-shirt was no longer white and looked like it never had been. It was covered in dirt, sweat, and dried blood. There was an IV in his left hand, the only clean spot there appeared to be.

Addy looked up at the paramedic, and he answered without a question. "He broke his leg, his femur."

"Praise God, I thought he'd been shot."

"So did we, when we saw all the blood on his clothes and all over his arms and hands."

Addy smiled at Red. "I'm pretty sure that came from the buck he must've just shot."

Red gritted his teeth. "It was a four-by-three!" His face was pale and wet with sweat. Shock had already set in.

Moving down the corridor, Red felt every bump and uneven tile his gurney could possibly hit. The hallway, never quite wide enough for modern equipment, seemed like it went on forever. Lights from above were intrusive and blotted out the faces of those looking down on him. He turned his head and faced the wall. He watched the horizontal black scuffs, bequeathed by the many gurneys before him, lead him farther into the hospital. Black-and-white photographs with cheap frames lined the wall above the scrapes and gouges—all men, probably hospital emeriti, long since living in a fancy retirement home. Or dead.

The emergency room was small and should've been quiet. The commotion of personnel bumping and moving equipment, combined with a need for urgency, made the room feel even smaller. He focused on Addy at the back wall. Her face fraught with worry, her hands clasped in front of her as if she had forgotten what to do with them. She watched the movement of the doctor and nurses. He could sense she was probably praying, too.

He wanted to tell her everything would be fine. He wanted to comfort her and say he was sorry for all the trouble he'd caused. He wanted to tell her how beautiful she was, and how much she mattered. She had changed his life, such a difference she had made. He wanted to ask her to marry him all over again. If he had a new ring, he would have done so right there. Addy's eyes turned to his. For a moment, they stared at one another, then she smiled. He mouthed, "Piece of cake." He was startled by his own words. *Are you kidding me? Piece of cake! That's all you got? Open your fat mouth and tell her you love her, at least. You old, stupid buffoon!*

Red turned and caught the doctor off guard. His face was full of tension. He gave out orders just short of shouting. Red liked the way the doctor called him "boss." Even with the perfunctory smile. "OK, boss, we got you. The worst part is over." Not too arrogant, and the slightly gray hair confirmed he was not too young. Probably never skinned a buck, though.

Red caught every other word or so. More blood. Dr. Whitlatch. Surgery. Stat. Panel. Artery. Loss. Nerve damage. Sounds were becoming muffled. Pain was finally easing. He looked at Addy and hoped it wouldn't be the last time. *Please, God, I don't ask you for much. Please don't let it be the last time.*

He woke up to Addy standing over him while singing his favorite Stuart Hamblen song.

She leaned down, her face close to his. He breathed in her perfume. Her lips were moist, and he thought he could taste the sweetness. She gazed into Red's eyes, moving hers gently from one to the other. She'd been crying. She cupped his forehead with her soft, warm hand.

"You're OK. The doctor put you all back together again, Humpty Dumpty."

Red smiled, closed his eyes, and asked, "Did I hear you praise God for my broken leg?"

Addy laughed. "Must've been the medication, my dear."

Red sat down on the grass. He rubbed his left leg and felt the hardness of the scar. The rods and pins were still deep inside. He could've lost his leg. He could have died. Red lay down on his back and watched the lullaby of the clouds moving overhead. He fell asleep and dreamt. It was the same hospital, the same incident, but he dreamt from a different perspective. The viewpoint of a ghost.

He saw himself lying on the gurney, heard the same conversation, but he was standing next to Addy. He saw himself being taken into surgery, but this time, he followed Addy into a small hospital waiting room. She was alone. She stood for a moment and her eyes panned across the sparsely furnished area: assorted magazines, a plastic plant, and ugly striped chairs surrounded by washed-out walls of beige.

Addy sat down and started to shake. Tears flowed from her eyes as she wept into her hands. She prayed. She prayed for Red and thanked God for bringing him back to her. She stayed there for hours, waiting and crying. All by herself.

Red wanted to reach out and hold her, to tell her he would be fine, but in the dream, he couldn't move. He felt her emotions wrapping around, penetrating his body. The worry she felt was more painful than the bloodied bone that protruded through his muscle and skin. Her love, profound and unyielding. He stayed by her side, invisible and helpless.

The doctor, still wearing blue hospital scrubs, finally greeted her. "He's gonna be fine, we think. He'll need physical therapy for a few months. It was a pretty severe spiral break. We have to watch for infection first, though. Get past that, and we're home free. Best case, you might notice a slight limp on his left side as he gets older."

Addy hugged the doctor, and he hugged her back.

Red woke from the dream. He ached at the pain—not at his own but Addy's. He never knew how scared she'd been, the sadness and worry he'd caused. Was it like that each time he'd left on his hunting trips? Did she worry about him when he was gone for days on end? He would've never gone had he known. She loved him so much, she'd never said a word about her burden. He wiped the tears from his eyes with the heels of his hands.

Over the next several days, Red and Jake crossed through a saddle between two mountains on the east side of the Sierras. Travel was difficult and slow, the terrain steep and the altitude high. They frequently stopped for rest and took short naps along the way among the open forest scattered with big ponderosas. The bark's yellowish-brown plates surrounded by black crevices looked like pieces of a jigsaw puzzle cleverly assembled to fit together perfectly. He picked off a piece of the bark and thought he smelled butterscotch.

Everything seemed to remind Red of his past life. Memories he hadn't thought of in years all felt like pieces of the puzzle connecting one with another. *Why am I having these dreams? Where are they coming from?* The dreams were taking him somewhere. His mind was alive, regenerated. He was being allowed to see his life as others had. *Are the dreams the secret, the way back home?*

Soon, he'd leave the land he knew so well and be in country far less familiar. "Jake, we better get this all figured out soon." Red looked down at the dog. "You know, you haven't been too much help deciphering things for us. Addy loved you, too. What'd she tell you? You're the one that's supposed to have all the senses."

Jake didn't comment.

They followed the contours downhill from the Sierras until he located the Susan River, which, in turn, led him to the north end of Honey Lake. The pines had turned to oaks, and then the oaks had turned to sagebrush. The lake area was full of wildlife, providing a perfect habitat for nesting and brood-rearing birds. Thousands of migrating, bounteous species, both in flight and on the ground. He watched a fierce fight between two red-eyed mud hens over nesting rights on a blob of floating weeds.

"Hey! You guys need to share."

Two northern grebes played on the surface of the water. Addy had always called the birds "Jesus birds" because they could walk on water—their courting ritual made up of head bobbing and a synchronized parallel run across the surface. Their harsh, screechy voices belied their beauty, making the Jesus thing a little suspect.

The next day, he followed the water's edge southward. At times, he and Jake would split thousands of birds as they walked through the lowland. The sound of flight was thundering. He felt like Moses parting the Red Sea. If only he could turn the water into wine. Occasionally, he left the lake area and followed game trails traversing south. He stopped and looked at some tracks in the dry mud under his feet. At first, he was confused and thought they must have been from Jake.

"Big, big dog tracks," he mumbled until he realized they were from a wolf. It was trouble, bad trouble, for both himself and his friend Jake.

Jake was absorbed in all the smells and marked at least five times in a fifty-yard circle with his tail held high. Red knew a hunting pack of wolves would be grueling to handle if they decided to come after his dog. They'd outweigh Jake by fifty pounds. Wolves were big, tough, lean predators and would not tolerate another dog in their territory. He looked at Jake and called him to his side.

He leaned over, hugged the dog, and promised, "I got you. I'm not gonna let 'em get us, my friend."

There were lots of deer, antelope, jackrabbits, and cottontails all around. He made sure he had plenty of wood to last the night and then went skinny-dipping in the lake. The sun set over the high mountains of the Sierras as he watched the desert hills to the east deepen from a dark-blue hue to almost purple.

Just after sundown, Jake fussed, then growled deep in his chest. In the distance, wolves surrounded the camp. Red grabbed on to Jake and tied him to a large log near the fire. For hours, the pack circled the camp, gradually coming closer, their presence only revealed by their distant reflecting eyes. Red removed the pistol from the holster and fired two times, killing a wolf with each shot. The remainder of the pack ran off into the darkness, leaving their dead at the edge of the firelight. Red kept Jake close to him for the rest of the night and didn't untie him until morning broke. Jake immediately ran out to the dead wolves. The wolves weighed well over 150 pounds each. Both were males and looked like two big dead German shepherds.

At the south end of Honey Lake, Red picked up the Long Valley Creek until turning east toward the Pyramid Lake area. At times, he found himself deep in thought and couldn't remember how long he'd been walking. Keeping track of how many miles he traversed over time was difficult. During the day, he kept his bearing with the sun, sometimes being surprised how long he'd been traveling. Time seemed to pass differently now, with miles crossed and not felt.

The occasional jackrabbit would bounce from its burrow and disappear to the east. He crossed over flat areas of the desert, cutting sagebrush with his hatchet for campfires. Sleep came in small bursts, between stoking the fire and the shrill sounds of coyotes and wolves.

The green sagebrush burned hot and quick, making the prep piles large and arduous to maintain. He learned to pick up wood along the way when getting close to a base camp, enough to make a good fire foundation. He let the dead wood burn down into a bed of coals and only added to the fire when he thought he heard an intruder. A round of sagebrush ignited into a ball of flames when thrown on the coals, the sound of the burst almost as intimidating as the blaze. He stared into the burning bush as if waiting for his message of pilgrimage. "I am burned but not consumed." The flames, just as quickly, disintegrated to ash, allowing the black night to reign again. Slightly jealous, still with no clear answers, Red silently conceded, *I'm no Moses.*

No. It was not the burning bush after all.

CHAPTER 23

The desert scenery was a pageantry of pastels. Waterless clouds were swept easily along by the wind, revealing stunning evening sunsets of unimaginable colors. Red looked at Jake lying next to the fire.

"It's pretty nice on this side of heaven, too."

Coyotes began howling at sunset. Their baying was now a sound that soothed rather than frightened. Bobcats, snakes, and finding sources of fresh water were the current conundrums. The next known water source on the map was twenty miles away. The jugs were full, and both dog and man carried as much of it as possible. "Please just let us get to the next watering hole." How he wished he could believe the water would be there for him when he turned on the faucet.

There were no trees ahead of them. The sunbaked sagebrush and rocks disappeared into the distant mirages of quivering air. Faraway dust devils were sporadic. Their movement looked like campfire smoke rising in narrow columns from the desert floor, each time leaving Red's heart beating faster than it should. Red and Jake walked for miles, and the landscape still looked the same. Surely, he wasn't walking in a circle. Red turned and saw the long, straight path of footprints he'd left behind. He confirmed with his compass.

"It's like we're on a treadmill, Jake. We're moving but not getting anywhere." He listened to his voice. It was better than silence.

"Did I ever tell you about the time I bought a 1965 Mustang? It had been sitting in an old lady's barn. She wanted to get rid of it, so she sold it to me for a thousand dollars. I thought I was helping her out. I didn't know much about cars. I wanted to help sell her property, so I bought the car, kind of as a favor. I turned around and sold it to a guy who was my friend. I didn't need it. Had my truck. Sold it to him for two thousand and felt kinda bad. Caspian Blue. Still had the barn dust on it."

Red stopped, caught his breath, looked at the dog, confirmed he was still listening, and continued with his story. "Alan Warren. That was his name. He turned around and sold it for seventy-five thousand dollars." He paused and looked out into the distance. "It was a Shelby." Four more steps. "I really don't like to talk about it."

They walked in silence until Jake paused, walked in a circle, and looked at Red. Red checked his compass again. "Are you lost or confused?"

The two boys sat at the kitchen table. George had the majority of the tabletop spread with parts of a disassembled radio. Each part was meticulously cleaned and placed down on newspaper in order. He unwrapped old black tape from the electrical cord and snipped the frayed wires. Red was sitting on the opposite side looking down at a book and a writing tablet in front of him. Red was more interested in what his brother was working on than the book.

"Red, you better get your homework done before Momma comes home."

"I hate this, I don't care about how many bushels of beans or how many ears of corn someone's got. Let's go outside, George, I can do this later. Just give me the answers, and then we can go hunting."

"We can't go until you're done, and I'm not giving you the answers."

The two boys continued with their respective tasks. Red looked at the parts in front of his brother.

"How did you learn how to do that?" Red asked.

"Well, sometimes you just got to jump in and tear stuff apart and then figure out how it's supposed to work."

"Then, can I help?"

"After your math problems."

George looked at Red's book and tried to read the question in the book out loud. "You know, Red, math can help you figure out how many boards you'll need to build your house or put on a roof. It can help you figure out the distance of the big buck you want to shoot and how you might need to adjust your aim or even what size bullet or shell you'll need. And if you go and sell something to somebody, you wanna make sure you're giving and getting a fair price on both sides.

"You can figure how much of something is yours and how much of something belongs to somebody else," George continued. "It's not only adding and subtracting, but it's also dividing, percentages, fractions, and multiplying. And just when you're about ready to figure all that out, holy cow, wait until they throw in that alphabet."

Red stopped, looked at George, and asked, "They throw in the alphabet?"

"Yeah, algebra. But you don't even wanna think about that right now."

Red continued with his homework for several minutes, then said, "I like reading. I like reading stories."

George put down his work and smiled. "Yeah? Reading and writing, well, that's what makes the world go 'round. How you gonna find out about other places to go and visit? How else would you know about stories about Scrooge or Tom Sawyer and Huck Finn, and what about Daniel Boone or even Hans Christian Andersen?"

"'I have never been lost, but I will admit to being confused for several weeks.' That's what Daniel Boone once said." Both boys laughed out loud.

"Why, maybe someday you can write a story about all the stuff we do and become a famous author. My brother, the famous writer."

"Yeah, I can write about all the times you were confused."

"We can do anything we want to do or be anything we want to be, if we work hard and never give up. You gotta study, even study the things you don't like, because someday they might just come in handy."

Red thought, *What could possibly be handy about a bushel of corn?*

"It's just like chemistry. I never liked it, but it turned out to be the best one of all. Chemistry is how cars drive and planes fly and rocket ships blast into space, and math gets them to where they want to go. Math and chemistry and physics are the only things standing between us and the moon. In chemistry, if you don't blow yourself up, the most important thing it teaches is that you never lose anything. Nothing ever goes away. Liquid can turn solid, a solid can turn to gas, and gas can turn to either one."

"So we shoot a turkey, the turkey turns into Thanksgiving dinner, we eat the dinner, and the dinner turns to poop."

"The point is, things always change, but we never lose anything. Once you understand that, well, you about got life all figured out."

"What do you mean?"

"Well, it's like love. You start out liking someone, and you may end up eventually loving them someday."

"Like when you get married?" Red asked.

"Yep, and you might not like somebody to start out with, then someday they might become your best friend. You never lose anything. It's all chemistry, the way I see it."

"What about when people die? If you never see them again, do you lose them?"

"Well, when people die, you don't stop loving them, you just have to love them in a different way, like in your heart and in your memories. They become a part of you, part of who you are."

"Like Daddy?"

"Yep, just like Daddy."

Red rechecked his direction, closed the compass, and placed it in his shirt pocket. His hand lingered close to his heart. He could barely feel it beating. How could one small organ be capable of so much resentment? And how could one small act, in a single moment, change the destiny of so many people?

>+++

Jake had become quite the bird dog, tail wagging as he ground-sniffed in a zigzag pattern along the way. He flushed two big sage hens from their hiding spots. The abrupt sound of their flapping wings broke the desert silence. Jake bounded after the birds but quickly lost the chase. The distinct odor of the bruised sage was a favorite, and Red gladly welcomed it.

Jackrabbits jumped every few yards, and soon, Jake paid little to no attention to them. Antelope stood guard from the top of every rise, and from a lower dry creek bed, a huge mule buck bolted out in front of them. The stag was out of place, and for a moment, Red thought it was a sign that he should shoot it for his food supply. But common sense prevailed. It was warm, there was no shade, and a fresh source of water was unknown.

Red watched the buck jump through the brush and softly said, "Go back to your family."

The day was warm and bright and uncomfortably hot. Red seemed to be more concerned for Jake than for himself, stopping every mile to give the dog a drink. Red squatted down and made sure Jake drank all the water that was given to him. Red looked over the horizon. He froze. His eyes widened, and he shot up to his feet like one of the prairie dogs Jake had been trying to catch.

He saw a small rise of campfire smoke in the east about a quarter mile out. This time, it wasn't a dust devil. It rose straight up, then dissipated into the air. He dropped his backpack but kept Stubs around his shoulder. He ran toward the column of smoke.

It had to be a human. *My God,* he thought. *A human who can tell me what's going on. Maybe I haven't lost my mind after all!* This human could tell him how to get back. Someone who'd been living on this side of the world longer than him.

Closer and closer. He tried to focus on the campfire. The running jarred his vision, and sweat fell into his eyes. He yelled as loud as he could. "Hey! Hey! I'm right here! Hey!" He waved one arm above his head and held on to Stubs with the other. Waving back and forth, he almost lost his balance. At any moment, he expected to see the human. He'd see the tent at least. It'd jut above the sage. Red stopped running. Hope fell from his face. His knees collapsed, boring into the ground. Steam was rising from a sulfur hot spring.

In that moment, the steam no longer resembled smoke. It was no longer his vessel home. It no longer held answers or even hints. It was but a bully toying with him, teasing incessantly. It rose above him, laughing.

Red stood. He was mad. "You bastard!" He raised Stubs and shot the rising steam. It made him feel better. He had been hoodwinked, duped. He wouldn't allow that to happen again.

Twenty miles later, it was late afternoon. The horizon shimmered and waved. Things appeared, then, just as quickly, disappeared, like a fine painter always making revisions with his oils. That's what he would do to pass the time. Of course, he'd paint Addy first. There, off in the distance, she stood, her dress moving with the breeze. She was walking toward him. She was carrying a platter of food. Fresh fruit and chocolate. He heard her voice. Her sweet, sweet voice. "Come, Red, let's sit still." She was so close. He could smell the fruit. It was red and yellow. Such a beautiful contrast against the desert. Red reached out, but Addy was gone. The canvas was only two colors now, blue at the top and beige at the bottom. He liked the blue better and took away the beige.

They crossed a wash, and in one of the small pools, Red topped off the water jugs, then took a bath with Jake. There were no trees, caves, or rock formations. But there was water, fresh and full of life.

As he was cutting sage, he disturbed a huge tarantula. He looked at Jake, then back down to the spider. "It's not bad enough that everything with fangs wants to eat my dog and me, but now steroidal spiders?" He killed the spider with a rock and continued reaping the sagebrush.

Long before daybreak, he and Jake were already afoot. The air was cooler just before the dawn. He could see a cluster of trees far off in the distance as the sun peeked over the morning horizon. He checked his compass and his position. The grove was in his direct eastbound route. It took several hours to reach the trees, and as they approached, he felt relieved after seeing a pond with fresh water. Two mallards circled above. Both descended and landed on the mirrored surface. Their calm bodies never revealed their laboring legs as they created ripples like those behind a child's little boat. Wrinkles on the surface of the water spread out and dissipated as they widened toward the edge. The pair were at peace, in their own perfect world. Red couldn't bring himself to kill the drake. He couldn't break up the pair.

Fish popped up as bugs skimmed across the surface. He retrieved his fishing line. After about thirty minutes of fishing, it was apparent Red would not be eating fish. He set the line down, whittled out a gig from a low-lying cottonwood branch, and speared five large bullfrogs. He had a fine creekside lunch of frog legs, lamb's-quarter leaves, and dandelions fried up in a pat of beaver oil. He pretended it was foie gras with duck rice, with the main course being duck à l'orange with Rouennaise sauce.

Red recorded his distance traveled in his logbook. *Approx. 21 miles/due east. Stupid sulfur spring dispatched. Bastard.* The feeling of being so close to finding another human was overpowering. He wanted to feel that emotion again. He couldn't imagine how he would feel when he found Addy.

Red packed up to leave, filled the jugs with fresh water, and placed the saddlebags on Jake. They traveled relatively danger-free for several days. He picked up the west end of the Humboldt River, which would take him all the way to Wells, Nevada, directly eastbound. He studied his maps and recalculated the distances traveled.

The river ran slowly. Its twisted course produced areas of marshes and pools, nurturing root vegetables and tubers along with an abundance of fresh berries and leaves for tea.

Red had prayed to escape bears, wolves, snakes, and even spiders. And that prayer had been answered with the introduction of his new nemesis: millions of mosquitoes. He traveled parallel to the river but at some distance, trying to avoid the confrontation.

Red didn't know what really attracted mosquitoes. His sweat, movement, sound, or all of the above. He pictured himself waking up with swollen eyes sealed shut with saucer-size welts. He felt his face and neck being penetrated by tiny little drills. He might die of anaphylactic shock, malaria, or even blood loss. His death certificate would be passed around the campfires by his drunken hunting buddies. *Cause of Death: Mosquito.*

Red fought with the nasty little bastards for several hours. A new cause of death: *Self-induced battery by means of slapping.* He retrieved the last tube of repellent, only applying it to Jake, specifically around his head, eyes, and muzzle. "Don't go getting any ideas I like you or anything."

Red pulled a pair of Addy's pantyhose from his backpack. Jake watched with concern. He cut off the bottom part of the leggings and used them as gloves while he wore the upper half over his head. It was probably a good thing he was alone in this world. Otherwise, he could've been arrested for suspected bank robbery. He looked hideous. Jake sat on his haunches and whined at his master's facial deformity. Red put on his backpack, checked his compass, and placed it back into his shirt pocket.

He walked past Jake and, without looking down, said, "Shut up."

CHAPTER 24

R ed fed the campfires green brush and decayed wood to produce as much smoke as possible. The desert was remaining hot even at night now. Both dog and man slept inside the tent. It was a sanctuary from the mosquitoes, except for the occasional interloper. Probably a scout, sent out ahead. Red had only planned to use the tent during the harsh winter months, but now it proved to be a valuable piece of equipment, literally worth its weight.

He was near Winnemucca. He'd have to cover more miles to beat the weather to the Denver cave. He passed an outcropping of rock within sight of the river about fifty yards away. It appeared to be a small cave beneath a tall, thin rock formation resembling a church steeple.

"Well, Jakester, it's not yet Sunday, so we'll keep on going."

It was early afternoon before they stopped to rest under the shade of a large cottonwood-type tree. Red hydrated himself and gave thanks for the water. Soon, he may not be so blessed. A breeze kept the mosquitoes away as Red fell asleep watching Jake chase after fish in the water near the river's edge. Jake moved and acted like a dog half his age. He sat in the water, motionless except for his eyes, with the water level halfway to his shoulders. As the murkiness began to pass, he followed the fish with only his head until he had a clear view beneath the surface.

With the movement and speed of a much younger dog, Jake jumped up and pounced on passing fish with his big paws until the assault disturbed the muddy river bottom, giving the fish their murky asylum again. Red didn't know how long he'd been asleep but wanted to at least get in another two miles before making camp. Jake was now lying by his side, keeping watch over the river. Red patted the dog's wet head.

Red put on his backpack, checked his compass bearing, and moved out. He stepped downward, his right foot slipped from a rock. His ankle rolled underneath his weight. Red screamed out in pain as he fell to the ground, then tumbled down the embankment. He fought to get out of his backpack and grabbed his lower leg. He had been wearing his tennis shoes to save the wear and tear on his boots. Now he regretted it.

"Are you kidding me! Are you freakin' kidding!" He took off his shoe and sock and examined his ankle. It was already turning blue. *How could I let this happen? I should've known better.* He winced in pain as he hobbled to the river. His ankle was swollen and getting worse. He finally limped back to his pack, found the first-aid kit, and took two ibuprofen, hoping it would reduce the swelling.

Red screamed. Cuss words came to mind. He slammed his fist into the dirt. He wanted to throw the ibuprofen bottle as far as he could, but then he'd have to go get it. He'd gone through so much, made good time, trekked so far. This one careless mistake could kill him. Now, with a hurt ankle, he'd be unable to travel. Time would not wait, seasons would continue, and winter would arrive. As long as he had water, he could survive the harsh, hot desert environment. But winter? Without shelter or heavy clothing, he would die.

He took the hatchet and crudely fashioned a crutch from a cotton-wood branch. It was obvious he couldn't walk and would have to camp for several days.

Red recalled the outcropping of rock about an eighth of a mile back. The cave would potentially be a good spot for safety. He was barely able to walk, let alone carry fifty or sixty pounds on his back. He dragged the backpack over to a rock, sat down, and rifled through the contents. He wouldn't need all of his ammo or his fishing rod at the cave. Nor his extra clothing, boots, and various other items and tools. He placed the extra ammo, miscellaneous equipment, and clothing in a bag, tossed a rope high in the tree above him, and hung the bag from a limb. The backpack was still too heavy to carry. He removed more items. Still too heavy. He fastened a short rope to the pack, relocated the Captain America shield to the bottom, and pulled the pack behind him. "Come on, Jake. Time to go to church, after all."

The cave was small and just barely big enough to sit or stretch out flat, but it'd provide excellent shelter on three sides, leaving him only one side to defend during the nights. He built a fire just outside the opening, organized his pack, and made up his bed. The location gave him a clear and unobstructed view of the river's edge. Other than fire-wood, which he'd need to gather, everything else was at his front door. It seemed the cave was meant to be.

He spent an uneasy night with his right foot elevated. It was awfully black outside, and the fire prevented any view past the fire ring. In the half-light of morning, Jake whined, a funny sound for him. He was standing at the edge of the cave with his tail curled high above his back. Red was wide awake at the first sound. He grabbed Stubs and looked out of the cave. At the very edge of the river, a reflection of eyes stood still. Low to the ground, they stared upward, toward the cave. Their size and stillness eliminated bears and maybe wolves. Jake was not in attack mode but rather had the look of a curious pup.

Red held on to the dog's collar and kept him inside the cave. By the time morning's full light arrived, the eyes and that which they were attached to were gone. Red hobbled down to the water's edge. He expected tracks, then scared himself when his mind began imagining finding a strange rune etched in the sand. A clue he'd need to decipher to get back home. There was nothing, not even in his imagination.

During the day, Red soaked his swollen foot in the cool river. He was able to shoot a small antelope that had come to water there. He buried the carcass in a hole he dug close to the water's edge in the soft dirt, hoping to conceal the smell. The antelope would provide food for at least four more days, along with a supply of meat strips he planned to salt and dry over the fire. It'd take three days to dry the jerky, between the sun and the fire. If he could make enough jerky and pemmican, time would be saved in the days ahead. With winter only a few months away, a single day may be the difference between life and death.

It took Red a full day to gather supplies. He used the Captain America shield to drag his full water jugs, firewood, and other needed items back and forth from the river to the cave. Between the trips, he nursed his ankle in the river. He tried to elevate his leg, but doing so consumed too much precious time.

Jake's ritual of whining to show his desire to play with whatever was calling him lasted for three more nights. Something had dug up the antelope's grave, and the carcass had been dragged away in the middle of the night. The ground was covered in a variety of tracks, maybe a wolf and lots of varmints. The eyes returned each night but left each morning as the sun emerged.

Red was moving about better than he'd expected. The bruising that had blackened the entire right side of his ankle and foot was almost gone. It was now just a faded, tender yellow reminder. The injury looked as if it was weeks old rather than days. Red rubbed his ankle and wondered if he'd miscalculated the time. Perhaps he'd spent several days passed out or in a delusional stupor. He rubbed his left thigh. His leg felt strong and firm. The old scar not painful at all.

Red was sure he'd spent five days recuperating. Five precious days that he would now have to make up while being careful not to reinjure himself. He taped up his ankle, packed up camp, collected a minimum supply of water, and headed east again.

The days seemed to pass by quickly, and soon Red forgot about his ankle. The river course was full of oxbows, which slowed down the flow of the water until it was almost stagnant. They kept their distance from the water's edge, only approaching it to resupply. Red knew the river flowed for miles and chose not to carry water. Crossing over the apexes of land between oxbows took hours, but the river always came back to them.

The nighttime visitor continued to appear for at least a week. During the day, Jake would often turn as if interested in something behind him. A bush would twitch, or Red would catch a fleeting blur of movement. It became more frequent as the days continued, until one morning, Red saw the creature for himself. It had taken cover behind a large pile of dead tumbleweeds about twenty yards away, only exposing its head. It was a coyote. She looked emaciated and near death. Her legs were long and her fur a light gray with a black-tipped tail.

She stood silent and watched the man and the dog. Her eyes were dull and soulless. She was not meant for this earth for too much longer. Her oversize ears moved individually, depending on her interests, with her large yellow eyes fixated forward.

Red smiled, looked at Jake, and asked, "Is that what you've been all twitterpated at?"

He took off his pack and removed a large handful of fresh antelope meat from the meat sack. He threw the slice underhanded toward the coyote, and it landed about five yards in front of her. She darted behind the brush and remained out of sight. Jake was beside himself over the next mile but finally gave up hope of ever meeting his new friend. Red hated coyotes but found himself looking back to see if she'd been following. A random thought entered his head. It was a verse he had heard when he was a child: *Do not forget to show hospitality to strangers.* It was an odd thought to have about a coyote, toward a species of scavengers and murderers.

Evening came quickly, and Red kept the fire small because of the warm weather. The coyote reappeared in the night and kept Jake awake until daylight. Red threw her some breakfast, which she reluctantly approached. It was the first time that she'd shown her full body. Her gait was awkward, as if she were hurt. She crawled until she reached the meat. With one swift swipe of her head, she and the meat were gone.

It wasn't until two days later that the coyote reappeared at the campsite. Red tried to control Jake as he threw out an entire ham of venison for the coyote. He pulled Jake back into his chest, and both watched the starving coyote devour its meal. She circled the camp, sometimes sitting and waiting, then moving to a new spot. Red was able to see her injury. Her right hind leg was shriveled. Part of it dangled. She'd obviously been hurt and couldn't hunt or feed herself. Her leg had healed the best it was ever going to, leaving, essentially, a three-legged dog.

This was a harsh, dangerous world for a crippled anything, human or animal. Other than starving, she'd adjusted to having three legs. She was balanced and spry but unable to run with any speed or agility. Jake was a big, strong dog, and Red had just about as much as he could stand of trying to control him. Jake was three times the size of the coyote and could defend himself in a fight. They were about to find out for sure.

CHAPTER 25

Red let go of Jake's collar, and the playful dog wiggled and pranced his way over to the coyote. Jake and the coyote went through the butt-smelling ritual, and, from Jake's display, Red had no doubt that Jake had found a girlfriend. The man threw out a handful of pemmican to the two dogs. The coyote grabbed the food, growled deep in her throat, and showed Jake her teeth. Jake could've cared less for her teeth or the pemmican. Red watched the dogs play and finally called Jake back to camp, leashed him up, and called it a night.

Red now had three mouths to feed. He felt useful again. Two dogs depended on his ability to provide food and water. But it was more than that. It was now a fellowship of kindred spirits. He shot a small deer near the water's edge. He gave the coyote a full ham. She ate an astonishing amount. Jake had no interest in the raw meat and waited impatiently to play. Red took backstraps, a ham, and two shoulders from the carcass. He put the meat in the sack and hung it in a tree, then bathed in the river.

It was clear the coyote was dying. Red had kept Jake on leash at night since the dog had befriended the coyote. Against his better judgment, Red wanted the coyote to stay, rather than take the chance that Jake would run away with her. The night was long, and Red dreamt of a different time, through his brother's eyes.

George sat across from Red. He was a good foot taller. Red's elbows were firmly planted on the top of the dinner table. George's mother placed the last bowl of food down and noticed Red's manners. She sat down between the boys.

"Red, I see you're all ready to say grace."

Red was oblivious to the etiquette lesson. "Thank you for our food and our day and for keeping everyone safe. We could use one more day without rain, but that's really up to you. Amen."

"Amen. Thank you. Pass your plate, please."

She dished up their plates and asked George how his day had gone.

"Pretty good. Mr. Dunbaugh said he could use help with his fence. I guess a string of barbed wire got loose and cut him pretty bad. Got infected. I can give him a couple hours after school."

"Make sure you don't expect anything in return."

"Yes, Momma."

"He's a good man. Let's keep him in our prayers."

Red didn't participate much. He looked distracted. Red surreptitiously took the biscuit from his dinner plate. He hid it in his handkerchief before asking if he could be excused from the table. George saw the whole thing, but their mother didn't.

"My, you must not be very hungry. Or is it my cooking?"

"No. It was really good, but I gotta meet for ball."

George knew something was up. Red didn't even play ball. Red had been acting a bit strange over the last two days, and this was proof something was up. George helped clear the table. Usually, both boys would run outside to enjoy the last bit of daylight. But doing the dishes put George in a perfect position in front of the kitchen window. George looked up and out the window as much as he could, trying not to tip off his mother. He was able to watch his cagey little brother.

Red quickly ran into the old woodshed behind the house at the edge of the woods. Within moments, Red reappeared with empty hands. It wasn't until well into the summer's night that George saw Red sneaking out the front door. From the darkened house, George watched his brother retrieve the handkerchief and biscuit. Red stuffed the hankie in his shirt and held a large flashlight in his hands as he sneaked into the woods.

George shadowed him at a distance and watched Red follow the path through the woods toward Blue's Pond. Red would stop intermittently, turn, and shine the flashlight into the forest. Each time, George would stop and duck down. Red looked around nervously. Maybe he heard a sound or saw a movement. He must be scared. George couldn't be sure.

Finally, Red veered off the path and walked to an outcropping of rock. He got down on his knees and crawled between boulders, holding the biscuit and flashlight out in front of him. George approached and saw that Red was at the mouth of a small rock den. Red softly called out to whatever was inside.

As the flashlight beam lit the inside, a large coyote screamed and hissed from within. It tore out of the den directly at the boy, who was frozen. George raised his rifle. He only had a fraction of a second to make the shot. He may hit Red, but if he didn't shoot, his brother would be attacked. He had to do it. He didn't have the time to think. A gunshot broke the darkness as the flashlight clattered down the incline. The coyote was dead but landed on Red. The boy screamed as he crawled backward on his hands and knees. George rushed to Red. His hand landed on Red's shoulder. George pulled Red back by his shirt, the material ripping. Red must have been even more frightened not knowing who or what was pulling on him. But George didn't have the time to explain. George's hand and forearm wrapped around Red's neck from the left. A rifle barrel to his right. Both stumbled backward away from the den and back down to the path.

"What are you doing?" George demanded.

Red couldn't talk. His mouth was agape, and any type of logical speech patterns were stuck somewhere between his mouth and throat. He wanted to say something, anything. But he needed to breathe first.

"What were you thinking, Red? Are you crazy or something?" George could barely see his brother in the darkness. He rubbed Red's arms and face, looking for a bullet hole, feeling for blood. "Are you hurt?"

Red could only muster "I'm fine."

George retrieved the flashlight and shook it, but it only worked intermittently. The walk home in the darkness was slow. Red explained he'd been feeding a young, sick coyote. "I never saw the mother before. I thought the pup lived in the den all alone." That sounded stupid. "I knew you'd be mad. I know how much you hate coyotes. I just had to do it. I'm sorry I scared you."

George didn't answer right away. He searched for the right words. How could he justify killing animals just for the kill? Red didn't have the guidance of a father. That had been taken away. But George had taken on the responsibility and sometimes hated it. Like right now. "It's not that I hate 'em. They're predators and kill anything they can. They'll kill our chickens and baby birds and even little fawns. And they can have rabies, so don't be so stupid."

"It was a pup, just a pup, and I was gonna train it to be our dog. I wanna dog so bad, but Momma always says we can't afford one."

George shook his head. "You could've been hurt real bad. Or maybe even me. Sometimes you can't listen to your heart. Your heart isn't smart. You gotta use your head. You can't tame wild animals, Red."

George grabbed Red by the arm and quickly turned him to face him. "Listen to me." His voice was direct and full of anger. "Coyotes are mean and are scavengers, and they'll never change."

Red jerked his arm from the grip and pushed George away. They were halfway back to the house, and all George could think about was whether his mother had heard the gunshot and what he was going to tell her. She'd probably be waiting on the porch, scared to death, wondering what had happened to her boys. He couldn't tell her what had really happened. It would scare her, and she would cry. It was all his fault. He should've stopped Red as soon as he'd left the house. He couldn't work out the words. He was angry. He was tired of being a father to someone who seemed to have no concern for anyone but himself. But George had made a promise.

"Red, have you ever heard of Aesop? Aesop's Fables?"

"No."

"Aesop had this story called 'The Scorpion and the Frog.' The scorpion asked a frog for a ride across the river, but the frog said no because he knew he'd get stung. But the scorpion promised he wouldn't kill him, because then they'd both drown. The frog thought about it. It made sense to him, so he let the scorpion get up on his back. 'Bout halfway across the river, the scorpion stung the frog, right in his soft underbelly. The frog was just beside himself, and said, 'Why'd you sting me? You said you wouldn't. Now we're both gonna drown. We're both gonna die!' The scorpion answered, 'It's just my nature.' That's the moral of the story." George stopped and grabbed on to Red's arm. "You can't change something's nature, Red, you can't tame wild animals. They are what they are. You coulda got hurt real bad."

Red was quiet the rest of the way home. The darkened house came into view. Red stopped. "You're saying it's the frog's fault! The scorpion saying it's 'their nature' doesn't make it OK."

"Shut up!" George whispered as loud as he could. "You're gonna wake up Momma."

"It's not the frog's fault. He was doing what he was supposed to do, helping someone out and giving the scorpion a chance. He trusted someone. It's the scorpion that needs its ass kicked for being greedy and wanting to hurt someone so bad that he'd just as soon die himself!"

It was past the point of a conversation or even an argument. It was bordering on a fight. Red clenched his fist. George had taken hits before without hitting back. But this time he'd fight back. Red closed his hands tightly, and George imagined that his fingernails were digging into his palms. George wasn't sure that Red had actually punched anyone before, at least not in anger. Red would probably aim for the face. No, Red was shorter and would go for the stomach.

Red burst out, "It's just like when Momma tells me about my temper, I'm the one responsible for it, and I'm the one who's supposed to change." His voice was loud and angry. George looked at the house. He was sure his mother would hear them now.

Red must have realized it, too. He gritted his teeth, restraining some of the sound. "So, the scorpion can change, too! That's the moral of the story, George!"

Red pulled back, preparing to throw a punch. George let his brother explode but now questioned whether he should've. Red's anger must have been all about trust. Trust, the most important of all virtues. Without trust, nothing else would be possible. Spit came through Red's clenched teeth as he yelled the last of his words. "You killed the baby's mother!"

George stood directly in front of him; the hit was coming. Red swung. The kitchen light broke through the darkness. George's eyes focused on the back door. What would he tell his mother? He felt the closed fist connect solidly with his midsection. Then another. Red hit so hard, George fell to his back. George looked up at his little brother. Red appeared shocked, his mouth open without words. Red turned in one quick movement and darted into the house.

The coyote kept her distance. Any sudden movements from Red caused her to flinch and retreat until she felt safe again. At night, Jake was kept tethered close by. Red could see the coyote in the firelight. Her head rested on her paws, and she looked to be asleep. When he woke, it was already daylight, and Jake and the coyote were sleeping side by side. Jake had chewed through the leash sometime during the night. Red was amazed that the two of them were still there. He called his dog, and Jake quickly obeyed.

The man scratched the dog's ears and patted his head. "Such a good boy, such a good boy." He hugged his dog as the coyote curiously watched.

Camp was packed up, and the journey continued. In the distance, flat buttes protruded out of the ground and reminded him of the back of a giant Rhodesian Ridgeback dog. To the northwest were massive pyramid-shaped mountains that looked like God himself had dropped piles of sand. The two dogs followed and played along the way. Red wanted the coyote to become tame, to remain with him and Jake. Chances were, Jake would follow her. But she needed food, and Red needed Jake.

He turned around and called out to them, "Come on, boy, come on, girl." She'd need a name. Aesop, maybe. "Come on, boy, come on, little lady."

For several hours, Lady showed no signs of wandering, and while she never got too close, she showed no fear of the man. When Red stopped, she stopped but never gave up her ground. She easily outlasted any staring contests and even appeared to challenge him on walking faster. Red finally got a closer look at her atrophied leg. It resembled an injury caused by a metal spring-trap.

Daytime was so quiet in the desert. About the loudest sound was his footsteps or the scratch of his pant legs against the sagebrush. Once in a while, a cast of hawks would screech, or he could hear the quack of a duck off the river flying overhead. At night, though, there was always the distant coyote, the owl, the whine of mosquitoes, the chirping of crickets, and maybe a frog or two.

The nighttime temperature of the desert was much different than the deserts of the Southwest. Red had been in the scorching Southwestern deserts and didn't care to return. They seemed to be a much harsher environment. Maybe those deserts were closer to hell. He missed his tall pines, the smell of fir, the sound of the wind through the trees and green; he missed seeing green. He'd be in the area of Wells soon, but for now, he found beauty in the distant juniper trees as well as the occasional faded cottonwood and willow next to the river.

He found creeks and springs all along the way, except for the last ten miles or so before he made camp. There were tules and cress in some of the ponds, and he got a much-needed change in diet. There were lots of ducks, quail, small game, and antelope. The only living things not moving east were the mosquitoes. They swarmed by the billions as if to let man know who was really still in charge.

Lady came closer to the man but still not within reach. Red wondered why she had not accepted his world as he had accepted hers. He'd only offered kindness and food, yet she, in return, showed such distrust. Why was she the only wildlife that seemed to be afraid? He held out a big chunk of red meat. "Come on, girly, I won't hurt you. Ask Jake, he'll tell you."

The coyote crawled nearer but stopped just short.

"Who hurt you so badly that you can't trust another soul?"

She laid her chin on her front paws and watched.

Red dropped the meat to the ground and placed his portion over the fire. He stepped away to pee. When he returned, his dinner was gone. Lady was at the edge of the fire's light and was just finishing it off. That had been the last of the meat! He looked out at the coyote and yelled, "Haven't you seen *Ol' Yeller*? Don't you know what happens?"

Later in the night, Lady scratched a bed in the dirt and curled up into a ball a couple feet away from the sleeping bag. She whimpered for Jake, who was on the bottom of the sleeping bag, sound asleep.

Red raised his head and looked at Lady, and she looked at him. "I'm not talkin' to you right now," he grumbled and then went to sleep with an empty stomach.

CHAPTER 26

Red looked at his map. The next hundred and fifty miles, he'd travel north into Idaho. The topography would allow him to bypass the major portion of the Rocky Mountains. They walked for seven hours with few stops, but there were five more miles to go to hit Red's daily goal. He had come so far and had conquered so much. Now, it was a race between him and the oncoming winter one more time. Addy was waiting for him. He would find her at Cabot Pond. Mother Nature would not win.

Red was tired and sat down near a willow tree and fell asleep. His nap was abruptly interrupted by Jake's barking. The dog was about thirty yards away, barking near a grove of young trees. It appeared Jake had cornered something, maybe another grouse. Jake snarled ferociously. It didn't sound like a harmless grouse. Red jumped to his feet, pulled Stubs to his front, and started to run toward Jake. The dog yelped in pain and burst out from the trees. The sound of his continuous cries was loud and full of agony.

Red ran after the crying dog. He had never wanted something to be over more quickly than Jake's pain, and at the same time, he didn't want to see what he might find. He grabbed on to Jake's collar and tried to settle him down. Jake's muzzle was laden with porcupine quills. Jake struggled to free himself. The quills pierced Red's hand and forearms. Red fought the impulse to scream out in pain. His teeth clenched and locked together. Jake was inconsolable. Red forced Jake to the ground and tied his legs together with the leather strap from Stubs. He tried to pull out as many of the quills as he could.

Jake's face was already engorged, his eyes swollen shut, and he whimpered with each tug to his muzzle. Red held tightly to the dog as he used the Leatherman pliers from his belt to pull out the last remaining quills. Jake continued to yelp and cry out, almost more than Red could stand. Lady circled closely and whined fiercely until Jake was back on his feet. Jake ran about, shook his head, and rubbed his bloodied muzzle with his front paws.

Red spent the entire evening comforting his dog. He applied a cool mud pack to his muzzle and forced a dose of tramadol down the dog's throat. He looked at his own hands, swollen, red, and painful. But he would save the pain medication for the dog. They finally lay down together and fell asleep, with Lady close by. Jake whimpered on and off and was restless throughout the night. By morning, the swelling had gone down, but it was obvious Jake was still traumatized.

As Red cleared camp, he looked at his pathetic dog and said, "See, Jake, we just have to learn how to live with the little pricks in our lives."

It took Jake a couple of days to get back to normal. Red was sure that Jake had accused him of causing all the pain, tying him up, and making him hurt even worse. It had been forty-eight hours since the attack, but in dog time, it calculated out to be three hundred thirty-six hours, or about fourteen days. That was plenty of time to have forgotten the entire incident.

Red washed in the river. He cut his hair as well as he could, parted it on the side, and called it good. He shaved his beard and left a neatly trimmed goatee, just like Addy had always liked. He was amazed that so much color had returned. He noticed the liver spots were gone from the backs of his hands and forearms. His wedding ring fit loosely, and he moved it to his index finger. He smiled at his ability to see so clearly up close without his glasses. His scarred leg was no longer atrophied, and he rarely found himself out of breath. He'd found his fountain of youth.

Red sat down and threw dead wood onto the fire. Lady came up and sat down next to him. He slowly moved his hand over to her face and allowed her to sniff and lick it. He lightly touched her head and scratched her ears. She quivered, and he felt her tenseness. Red admired her courage.

He moved his hand away, and she lay down with her head on her paws. Red had two best friends: Jake on one side, and Lady on the other. Tears came into his eyes as he thought about his life. He had never been so thankful for so little in all of his life.

They followed the river for several days. The water overflowed at every low spot, creating a long series of sloughs and branches that harbored nasty flying pests and horrid amounts of mosquitoes. The wetlands were huge and in places looked to be a mile wide. Red believed the river was soon to break to the north. It would be the turning point for Idaho. The north side of the river had firm ground. He'd follow the Humboldt to the head, continue north to cross over Thousand Springs Creek, and then pick up the Salmon Falls Creek.

Red made his usual raft with the inner tube and secured his belongings on top. This time, however, Jake would need help. Red emptied out all of the water jugs and canteens and secured the tops back on tightly. With his belt and some parachute cord, he strapped the empty containers around Jake's rear underbelly, leaving his legs free. Jake wasn't impressed. Red picked up the dog and the string of jugs and placed it all into the river. The containers popped up on either side of the dog and lifted his hindquarters to the surface.

The two crossed the water with Jake closely tethered. Jake was beautiful, a sight to behold. He floated across the water with the gracefulness of Esther Williams in a black-and-white movie. He negotiated through the current with the navigational prowess of a river otter. Love finally overtook Lady, and being reunited with Jake was her only concern. Once she was in the water, she was direct and focused.

They broke the river's edge, rested, and dried out. Elevation was around five thousand feet and would keep within that range for many miles. The weather was tolerable, but the nights were turning cold. He'd now have to keep more detailed calculations. He wasn't familiar with lower Idaho.

Red crossed into a dry ravine. It was about twenty-five feet deep, rather steep, and layered with shingled rock. Shale broke away and skated down beside him. He had made it up the other side, almost to the top, when he lost his footing. The weight of the backpack flipped him over. He slid on his belly, head first, down the ravine. He kept his eyes closed. He didn't want to see the injury. His head hit the bottom. Rocks and dirt continued to fall after he stopped moving. He landed upside down with his feet pointed up the bank.

Red couldn't move his legs. But there was no pain. *I'm paralyzed! I broke my back.* There at the bottom of the ravine, unable to move, he would starve to death. He'd be eaten alive by wild animals, unable to defend himself. Animals would tear at his muscles and innards. They always go after the innards first. He wouldn't feel the pain, but he'd watch himself bleed to death.

His hands had feeling. He could move his hands! Abrasions on both palms. He was moving his arms. He tried his legs again. Nothing. He wanted to look. The twisting of his head could finish him off. They said to keep your head still, immobile. But he wanted to see. He moved his head slowly, twisting to see his legs. The backpack pinned his legs tightly against the shale. He needed to move the pack. He could move his foot, which was under a loose pile of rock, but nothing else. He pulled at the pack, then pushed it aside. His legs were moving now, first one, then the other. Nothing was paralyzed, nothing broken. *Oh, thank God!* He was more thankful that there had been no witnesses. He felt like an idiot. How could he let his paranoia take so much control? He lay his cheek flat against the ground and gathered his thoughts.

As the dust settled, Jake sat down next to his face. Red could only see Jake's big front paws. The man could not decide whether the dog was there in support or to laugh at him. A rock about the size of a baseball finally stopped rolling when it landed on the side of Red's head. His vision distorted, like he was looking through a fish-eye lens. Red crawled up to his hands and knees. He picked up the rock, examined it, and said, "Look, Jake, no moss."

They camped within eyesight of the river. Red studied his map and looked at his compass. The compass had belonged to his father, the father that he'd never known. He could barely remember what he looked like from the old photographs his mother had given him long ago. He held the compass up to his face, closed his eyes, and breathed in, hoping for a trace of his father.

George sat at the kitchen table as Red sat next to him doing his homework. George was looking at a map and holding a compass in his hands.

"George, how can you look at that compass and then look at the map and put them all together?"

"Get your homework done, then I'll show you."

"It's all math, isn't it?" Red was done studying.

"Yep, I'll show you." George spread the map out over Red's school papers and started the math lesson. "Well, remember when I was telling you about fractions and parts? Compasses, no matter what size they are, all have degrees, kinda like parts.

"The compass kinda looks like a clock, but instead of time like seconds and minutes, it's degrees. Three hundred and sixty." George pointed to the face and explained the needle and magnetic north. "The top of the map should always be north, so if you match up the compass's north to the map's north, that's how you start. See?"

"That's easy, but I just remember where I've been and know where I want to go, all in my head."

George agreed, "Or just do that."

"That's Daddy's compass, isn't it?"

The older brother nodded his head.

"It's all simple to me."

George pulled back and laughed. "OK, I guess I don't have to explain compass declination, then."

Red placed the compass back into his shirt pocket and buttoned the flap. He watched the dogs play and thought about his brother. It had been decades since his brother's death, but there was a part of Red that would never believe George wouldn't come running back with some elaborate joke. Most of his life, Red had tried to suppress the memories. He considered himself good at concealing his emotions. The terrible pain lingering for years just behind his eyes. When he was young, he'd thought the agony would last forever. A fourteen-year-old boy trying to process so much pain and loss. He'd known his life would never be the same. But George was right. The heart-wrenching grief eventually changed, was repressed into a hollow space and wrapped tightly deep inside.

The two boys were wrapped warmly in their worn coats and boots as they walked through a sparse forest of oak trees intermixed with an occasional pine or fir. Each had a rifle, and Red led the way. Red's copper hair stuck out from underneath his cap and covered the top of his ears. Each boy looked forward, the vapor from their breath barely visible. Red stopped abruptly and lifted his rifle in aim.

"Wait, Red, wait for me, don't shoot yet," George whispered from behind. "Where?"

The rifle appeared oversize as Red aimed it forward. "Right there, George."

"OK, wait a minute. Lean up against this tree and get a good sight. Remember, that gun is really gonna kick."

The forked-horned buck was small.

"Hold your breath, then squeeze the trigger."

A large boom filled the forest. The rifle kicked back, and the back of the scope hit Red's right eye. The pain was enough to make him instantly start crying. George grabbed the rifle from Red's hands, and Red covered his eye.

"Let me see, Red," George said.

Red's eyebrow had already started to swell. A goose egg, for sure.

"You're OK, Red, it just kicked a little. Let's go get your buck." George carried both rifles and followed behind Red.

Red was still shaking off the sting on his face. He could feel the swelling but was too distracted by his excitement about the buck. He'd worry about what to tell his mother later. They reached the area near where the deer had been standing.

"Was he right around here, Red?"

"Yeah, right here by this brush and stump."

George leaned toward the ground and said, "Good job point-fixing the spot. There's a bit of blood right here."

Red looked intently at the ground and added, "Right here, too, and broken brush right over there."

Red slid down a hilly area deep with forest compost until he found another spot of blood. George could barely keep up with Red, and soon both were breathing hard and trying to catch their breath.

Red saw the buck lying down at the base of a large pine and yelled, "There he is!" He took off running as fast as he could.

"No, wait, stay with me."

But Red was already yards ahead. The buck surprisingly jumped to its feet and ran over the next ridge. George caught up to Red, and both examined the spot where the buck had been lying. A large amount of fresh blood was on the ground, and it was obvious the buck wouldn't survive.

"Damn it, Red, I told you to stop. You can't do that, you have to wait and take another shot. We coulda had him by now."

After two hours, the boys finally found the buck. The animal was dead.

By then, they were over the ridge, deep in the forest. Red's eye was black with bruising, and his eyebrow sported a large goose egg swell. They field-dressed the buck, packed up the meat, and headed home. It seemed they had walked for miles, with Red constantly talking. George carried both rifles and most of the meat. They were taking numerous breaks now, with George looking in each direction.

"George, are you lost or something?"

"No, I'm not lost! It's just a bit more."

Red continued to ask questions. Before George could answer, Red would be talking about something else. "I'm getting awful hungry."

George removed a cloth from his jacket pocket. "Here, eat the rest of the crackers."

Red devoured the crackers. It was the only time he didn't talk. George shook the canteen and handed it to Red.

"How much longer, George?"

"Just a few more miles, then we'll be home."

The two continued, but Red was slowing down. George looked around. He slipped and fell. Both guns hit the ground. Red stopped. He had never seen George be careless with the guns. In fact, he had never seen him act so strange, so tired he was breaking a sweat.

Darkness would be coming, and that was not good. George turned directions. Red was pretty sure they'd passed over the same area before. "George, are you scared of what Momma is gonna say about my eye? Does it look that bad?"

"I ain't scared, but it does look kinda bad."

"Then why you acting so funny? I think we're going in circles."

"We're not going in circles, and I ain't acting funny. I'm just figuring out what to tell Momma and not lie about it. Now, shut up, already. Let's just take a break right here," George said as he sat on a downed tree.

Red took off his meat pack and drank the last of the water. "I'm tired of scouting around. Let's just go home now."

George turned and looked in different directions.

"I'm starving, George, and if you don't want me to start eating this buck raw, you better come, too." Red put on the meat pack, turned to his right, and walked away.

George didn't say one word but followed his little brother. After less than a half mile of traveling in a near-perfect line, they were home, and Red had never stopped talking.

Red smiled and thought of the hundreds of times throughout his life that he had been the guide on hunting trips. He'd always been blessed with a strong sense of direction and intuition that others claimed he took for granted. Addy called it his "natural magnetism."

Both dogs were gone. Red had been deep in thought and had lost track of time. He jumped to his feet and called out to Jake. Red hurried to the top of the dry knoll. After several more calls, Jake came bounding over a small rise.

"Where's Lady?" Red promptly walked in the direction that Jake had emerged from. Red didn't want to lose her, although a coyote was a wild animal and couldn't be tamed. She needed to be in nature, with her own kind, anyway. But now she'd become a part of Red's family. He had welcomed her in, fed and nurtured her back to health. She had been their friend. They had trusted one another and had become a pack. Red crested the rise.

No, it was he and Jake who were in the wild; they were the intruders within her environment.

CHAPTER 27

It couldn't have been more than minutes. The dogs had just been there, playing. Lady couldn't have gotten far. He heard an animal cry and found the coyote stuck in a large round of sagebrush. Her flopping leg had gotten wedged in a fork. She chewed at her foot, trying desperately to free herself. Red took his knife from his belt. Rather than cutting the brush, he quickly swiped at the dangling tendon and cut off the atrophied foot. She yelped and ran off. Red was concerned how long, in dog years, it'd take her to forgive him. She stopped on the hillside, licked her stump, and quickly returned to camp with her pack.

The coyote was much heavier now and, other than her missing leg, looked healthy. Her fur was thick and glossy, her eyes sharp and bright. She hunched over her meat like a miser, bolting chunks of meat, snarling and growling. Poor Jake didn't know what to make of her but always gave her a wide berth at dinnertime. At dark, the coyote lay down close to Red's bed and slept most of the night. They were indeed a pack, an oddly blended family living as one.

The walking was easier along the many game trails near the water's edge. The population of lizards, rattlesnakes, and other unwanted reptiles and serpents seemed to suddenly increase for some reason. The dogs instinctively kept their distance during such encounters but could move much faster than the man when invading slithering reptile territory. For the most part, the rattlers just slithered on their bellies and flicked their forked tongues. Only when annoyed did they coil, raising their tails with a slow twitch, preceded by a rattling blur just before the deadly strike. But now, no one was left for them to hurt. Red left them to their lonely, miserable lives.

Sunsets in the desert were spectacular. The entire sky turned to electric pinks and blues, each one with its own unique canvas. In the afternoon, unexpected clouds formed and produced a soaking rain well into the night. The fire struggled to keep a flame and needed constant fuel. Red was tired and went to bed as soon as the sun was down. Both dogs curled up close and never moved until daylight. By morning, the camp was a mess. Everything was wet and muddy, including the dogs.

The rising sun warmed the desert. Steam rose from the wet earth, forming a shallow stratum of vapor that lolled across the desert floor. As they traveled north, the terrain didn't noticeably change, except the river began to be bordered by higher desert walls. They left the security of following the Humboldt at its head and went in search of Salmon Falls Creek.

Throughout the days, Red was lost in thought, and before he realized it, each day was over. He'd stop along the way, turn around, and have no recall of what he had just passed.

They picked up the Salmon Falls Creek about halfway between the Humboldt River and the Idaho border. The creek, more like a river, was a welcome change. The water's edge turned from fringed edges of rock and sagebrush to green borders of lush grasses. Red figured he was halfway to Denver, and it was getting close to midsummer. The territory along the river provided plenty of food and water, but his main concern was reaching the Denver cave.

They continued north on Salmon Falls Creek to the Snake River confluence. Although he had never been to the area, he knew his exact coordinates, and that gave him solace in his solitary world. At times, they stayed at the river's edge but other times had to climb out from the canyon and follow the river from high above on plateaus that stretched out endlessly. In places, the river was bordered by high, rocky cliffs with large mounds of scree at their bases. The combination of horizontal colors from the blue sky and sharp tan cliffs and a peaceful blue river below, trimmed in lush green on either side, looked like an oil painting conjured up in someone's mind. The skies were a brilliant blue that looked so wide and panoramic, it was nearly impossible to take it all in.

The grass was knee deep and unyielding in its expansiveness. He approached the edge of the massive cliff and looked beneath him. A strong breeze from below brushed him back with cool air, as if to keep him from taking another step closer to the edge. He watched an eagle fly below, tailing the course of the river, looking for prey or maybe just enjoying its freedom. Red was standing before majesty that his eyes couldn't believe. He stood above where eagles flew. He had the view of God. This was how the land was intended to be.

Never before having the view from above, Red watched the eagle soar effortlessly. He could see a large herd of elk far below in a wide grassy area between the river and the cliff. He looked deeper, farther, squinting for better vision. The herd was not elk but buffalo. He quickly grabbed his binoculars and looked at the herd for several seconds. He dropped to his belly at the edge of the cliff and looked through the lenses. The herd consisted of hundreds of bulls, cows, and calves feeding and playing in the deep-green swards. A rout of wolves patrolled the edge of the herd like sheepherder's dogs, except they were looking for the easiest kill.

Red rolled to his back and placed the binoculars on his chest. He needed a moment to process. He wondered what mixed-up events could make his mind conjure such sights. He had tried so hard to navigate through this world, to listen to the clues, to find his way back from his decaying mind. It must be a simple act transformed into his new reality. He must be in a car, Addy taking him for a drive. A field hawk transformed into an eagle, a herd of Hereford cows interpreted as buffalo, all surrounded by a warm breeze coming through the open car window.

He picked up his equipment and moved about a hundred yards away from the top of the cliff. He took off his shirt and removed Jake's saddlebag as well. Red allowed his dogs to run free with abandon while he laid out his sleeping bag, crushing down the tall grass beneath it. He breathed in the fragrance of the bruised grasses. He held out his arms and tilted his head back and looked up at the sky. He softly closed his eyes, turned gently, and felt the warm sun on his skin. He slow-danced in rhythm to music that wasn't there. Surely, he thought, he was in a dream. He opened his eyes and looked out over the land.

"Well, Addy, we finally have our open concept."

The dogs played in the distance. He lay down on his back and watched the white puffs of clouds. The tall surrounding grasses barely swayed, while the clouds overhead stirred themselves into colliding likenesses of rabbits, dragons, cars, houses, and ocean waves. That was what his mind was doing, too. Thoughts and patterns and random data observed through the filter of pareidolia.

Jake returned from his romp and sat down next to Red. The dog tilted his head back and forth, as if trying to understand why the man was sleeping in the middle of the day. Jake licked Red's face to no avail. Jake lay down and placed his head on the man's chest.

By late afternoon, they'd gained several more miles. Red heard the crashing water of Shoshone Falls long before he viewed its thundering power. The river dropped over two hundred feet straight down after cascading through the sharp canyon cliffs and stretched nearly nine hundred feet across the entire gorge. The deafening waterfall lured him to the water's edge. The power and force of the flow were mesmerizing. How easy it would be to take one more step, falling with the water and being quickly churned, never to return to the water's surface. He would feel no more pain, no more loneliness, and no more sadness. He needed to step back, break the hypnotic trance. *Just give me a sign.* Jake licked his hand and nuzzled into his side. Red shivered, his stare broken.

Red patted Jake's side. "We'll be OK. Let's go up top." But the falls were so loud, he couldn't hear his own voice.

He made camp about a half mile upriver from the falls on the plateau above the gorge where he could see for miles in all directions. The evening was quiet except for the lulling hum of the river below. The occasional shrill yelp from a prairie falcon overhead reminded him of a time long ago.

A large bird flew overhead and called out as Red and his mother walked into town. "Look there, Red," his mother said, "look at that beautiful bird. Just imagine what it can see. It's following us."

"Why's it doing that?"

"To make sure we're OK. That's what falcons do, son. He's the king of all birds. When they follow you, it means you'll be safe."

"I think it means he's hungry or he doesn't like us."

Red's mother slowed as she walked past the haberdashery of store supplies on the sidewalk in front of Mr. McAdams's general store, eyeing things she couldn't buy. She hesitated in front of the closed door and purposely waited for her lollygagging young son. "Red?"

"I got it, Momma, I got it." Red rushed past her and opened the screen door.

"Well, thank you, young man. What a gentleman."

He smiled as two older ladies on the sidewalk looked at his mother. Their heads leaned together as one covered her mouth with her hand while she whispered. Red tilted his head as he watched the women. Red's mother took her son's hand, smiled at the women, and pulled him into the store.

Once out of view of the nattering women, Red's mother paused. Her smile left. She breathed in, straightened her dress that didn't need to be straightened, and looked at Mr. McAdams.

Mr. McAdams, always kind, always genuine. "Afternoon, missus, what can we help you with today?"

She searched for words, looking embarrassed. "I . . . forgot."

Mr. McAdams's wife stood on the opposite side of the store. She imitated a smile, but her eyes did not. "Mrs. Johnson." *Mrs. Johnson,* period—she couldn't be bothered with anything more. She subtly waved at the women on the sidewalk, then returned to cleaning the glass-topped counter.

Mr. McAdams gave his wife a look of frustration. His voice slightly ringing, he said, "Ruth." He stepped from behind the counter. "Don't worry about those things, Mrs. Johnson, those old biddies have nothing else in their lives."

Red stepped up and proudly said, "Momma, we came here to get some flour and sugar and to look at the new BB gun. Remember?"

Red's mother managed a kind smile. "I know what they're saying." Red's mother looked out the door and then back to Mr. McAdams. "Don't you think I know what people say in this town?"

Mr. McAdams gathered the items from behind the counter while making small talk. Then he directed Red to the glass counter display case. A brand-new BB rifle! Wood stock and all.

Red ogled the BB gun behind the glass. That's what he wanted to look at. He knew better than to touch the glass. It was so close, nearly in his hands.

Mr. McAdams quietly smiled. He leaned over the counter. "I know, Mrs. Johnson, but there's a lot of good here, too. You know that I think the world of you and the boys. And other people do, too." He bagged the goods. "Sometimes you just have to wait for people to figure out they're not sheep and they're obliged to think for themselves."

She smiled, paid for her groceries, and pulled Red away from his fixation on the display case.

Red took the items from his mother's arms, turned, and looked at Mr. McAdams and promised, "I'll be back when I can, Mr. McAdams. Don't you dare sell it!"

Mr. McAdams started to follow Red's mother to the door. "If there is anything I can do for you or the boys, you just let me know."

Red's mother turned, looked at Mr. McAdams, and smiled kindly. "Thank you."

The screen door squeaked as it opened, then slammed closed with a sharp thud as Red and his mother left the store.

After Red had thoroughly concocted a plan to pay for the gun, he thought about the women on the sidewalk. Strange how they'd seemed like they were laughing at him and his mother. And Mrs. McAdams's snarkiness. Maybe Mrs. McAdams was just having a bad day. Red wasn't supposed to hate people. He hadn't walked in her shoes, after all. But he didn't want to. He didn't like her.

CHAPTER 28

The memory of the visit to the general store with his mother was still fresh. Red never understood why his family moved so many times, but he always appreciated the experiences later on. He thought of another time.

Inside the house, Red was impatiently waiting for George to get home from school. As the back door slammed, Red walked toward the kitchen and saw his brother stomping through the room.

His mother called out, "George!"

Red knew something was wrong. George immediately walked to the kitchen sink and began to wash his face and wipe away the blood from the corner of his mouth. George's shirt was torn and stained with dirt and grass. Red abruptly stopped and watched from the living room.

"What happened, George?" his mother asked.

"Nothing, Momma, nothing. It don't matter anyway."

She took George by the shoulders.

His face was red, and it was obvious he'd been crying. George turned his head to avoid her look. "It's all lies again, Momma. It's all lies."

His mother pulled him into her and hugged him before pushing him back and looking directly into his tear-filled eyes.

"George, I will not let this happen again." She wiped his face with a dish towel. "No more."

The next day, they were packed and moving to a new town.

The vast rolling prairie was full of antelope, deer, and elk. Cottontail rabbits were stirred up from their burrows by the dogs, along with an occasional red fox. Each day, the dogs would go for their morning promenade and play and wrestle. They made Red feel young again. Two dogs now. Something he was never able to have as a kid. Red never realized, until he was an adult, how poor his family had been. Never able to afford a dog and barely able to pay the rent.

"It's all fun and games until someone ends up in a cone," he yelled.

He played with Jake, and both entered into a game of chase. Lady watched but was hesitant to participate. Finally, she joined and chased after Jake. She hit him broadside, knocking him end over end but leaving her unfazed.

Red laughed out loud and yelled, "Come on, Jake, get up! Five-second rule, five-second rule."

Jake popped back up, oriented himself, and ran after Lady as if the collision hadn't occurred.

Over the next several days, he followed the Snake River until it turned discernibly north. Red continued east until he believed he was near Pocatello. Then, in the Soda Springs area, he picked up the Bear River. He reevaluated his original plan of finding the Sweetwater River. He worried he'd have trouble crossing the Bridger-Teton area. He worked his maps and compass calculations over and over. He was confident in his distances, mileage, and coordinates but had lost track of the days. If winter set in early, he'd be doomed without shelter.

They walked through a hillside of tarweed, a grayish-green plant with sticky little yellow flowers. Jake's muzzle and entire underbelly were greasy with the tar. He fussed and pawed at his muzzle and sometimes sneezed when it was unbearable.

"Bless you," the man told him each time.

The tarweed didn't wash off easily. Water had to be heated to dissolve the tar from Jake's thick coat. He got most of the smell and tar off with warm water he heated up over a fire. Red felt a lump behind Jake's ear. A tick!

"You little bastard."

Ticks were hideous and right up there with mosquitoes as unnecessary and pointless creatures. They weren't even worthy of the title. They were organisms. Red shuddered at the thought of a tick embedded in his body.

"Please, God, if I have to have one of those little bastards, at least put it where I can reach it."

That night, he checked himself out thoroughly before getting in his sleeping bag. When Red was almost asleep, he sat up with a big, loud sneeze. Jake was startled awake and stared at Red. Red looked at the dog, waited, then questioned, "Bless me?"

But the dog refused.

Time was now his biggest concern. He moved south until he was in the area where Highway 30 used to be, which would lead to the Green River stretch. The route was part of the Old Oregon Trail and a railway line. The route would bypass all of the high-peaked mountain ranges and snow areas, winding its way through valleys, passes, and mountain saddles. It'd save him days and maybe his life. He prayed he had made the right decision and pretended to have faith.

He crossed through spectacular green valleys of sage, grass, and scattered juniper trees backed with foothills that led into snowcapped mountain peaks far off in the distance. He felt insignificant as he looked toward Oxford Peak towering into the southern sky, the last of its summer snow glistening in the afternoon sun. Its jagged edges made the rolling grass- and sage-covered foothills look soft and inviting. But up close, the sage was thick and rough.

His pants were torn and needed constant repair. Jake had to be brushed nearly every evening, checked for cuts and ticks. The prairies were swept clean with wind and rain, as they probably had been since the beginning of time. It left an unobstructed view of feeding antelope and elk as far as the eye could see.

The valley was striking and pristine. Small cottonwoods and brush dotted the banks of the Portneuf River as it meandered through the foothills and intertwined through neighboring mountain ranges. Bursts of rain slowed him down. He hadn't planned for delays. He was already behind in his calculations. He had to push on.

Red was through the Bear Valley and over the Georgetown Summit. He made camp near the river but far enough away to avoid any potential nocturnal encounters at the local watering hole. Antelope were plentiful and would be on the menu for the next several days. As Red harvested a kill, the bloodied knife slipped and cut deep into his left thumb, down to the palm. He encouraged the bleeding to help clear the wound, then wrapped it tightly with his bandana. After the bleeding slowed, he sutured the cut with fishing line. He left one end of the skin slightly open for drainage and wrapped it up. He'd have to keep it clean. If infection set in, there would be no means of treatment. He could die of gangrene, a hideous death, right up there with black-widow and snake bites.

He put the last bit of wood on the fire. His body was tired, his thumb throbbed with every heartbeat. Red thought of his family and all the different places that they had lived. He counted in his head, trying to tally it up.

George and Red stood across the street from the school. Both boys were dressed in their best clothes. Red's hair was neatly combed, and it was obvious it had been parted on the side for the first time in a long time. George licked his fingers and tried to flatten a reluctant piece of Red's hair on the back of his head.

"I don't want to go to a new school, George," Red said as he looked at the students across the street.

"I know, but sometimes we ain't got much of a choice."

"Why do we always have to move?"

"Tell you what, I saw a new place we can go hunting, just outside of town. We'll go there right after school, OK?" Red looked past George toward the front doors of the school. "Look here, Red, take your hands and put them together like this, like you're about to say your prayers." George placed his writing tablet between his knees and held his hands out in front, palm to palm. "Now interweave your fingers like this."

Red copied his big brother and held his interlocked fingers tightly together.

"Now that feels normal, right?"

Red nodded.

"Now point your fingers straight up and move each finger on your right hand one position down, like this. Now that just feels strange, don't it?"

"Yeah, it feels wrong to do it that way."

"It's not wrong. There's no right or wrong way about it. It feels different until you get used to it. It's just another way of doing things. And that's what going to a new school is like. It feels different just for a little while, but before you know it, everything's gonna feel the same again."

George folded and crossed his arms in front of him and said, "Here, try this one." He crossed his arms opposite of how he'd first had them. "See there, ain't nothing wrong with either way. It just feels funny."

Red laughed as he practiced changing his folded arms back and forth.

"That's all you gotta do, Red. It's OK to feel different sometimes. If you didn't feel different or scared or worried once in a while, you wouldn't know how nice it is when you don't."

Red smiled. "OK, let's try out the new hunting place right after school."

As the two boys walked across the street, George whispered, "Just promise me one thing, Red, don't be getting any girlfriends on the first day. They're not coming hunting with us."

Red cleaned up camp and washed up the best he could with his disabled thumb. The sleeping bag was comforting, and it felt good to lay down. The deep cut on his thumb throbbed with any movement. As he looked at the wound, Red put the palms of his hands together and slowly interlaced his fingers. His life, now, was definitely different. He couldn't have his brother back, and maybe he would never have his life back, either. Red fell asleep under the night sky and dreamt through his mother's eyes.

The office room was small, dingy, and cluttered. Old, dusty trophies were atop a wooden file cabinet behind the oversize desk. Red's mother was sitting in an uncomfortable small wooden chair. Across the desk, a man sat facing her. His chair squeaked with his weight. Strands of greasy hair were combed over his balding head. He adjusted the nameplate at the front of his desk. *Principal.*

The man leaned forward with his hands folded on top of the desk among stacks of files and assorted papers and said, "Mrs. Johnson, you know we like you and your boys. But George, well, he just can't get along with the other boys. Someone is going to get seriously hurt now. I'm sorry, Mrs. Johnson, we can't take him back."

Red's mother was obviously upset, but her natural kindness prohibited her from being anything but polite. She stood, shook the principal's hand, and said, "I understand." She didn't say another word until she got in the driver's seat of the car.

George was impatiently waiting in the passenger seat. He didn't look at his mother but said, "Momma, I'm sorry."

She started the car, then paused. "This has to stop. Why is this happening?"

George looked down and didn't say a word.

"George, tell me. Now."

"The kids were mean, they said Daddy was a coward. They said Daddy killed himself because he didn't love us." George paused, catching his breath. "They said that we were devil kids."

Tears fell from his mother's eyes. "George, you know your daddy loved you. He loved us more than anything in the world."

"I know, Momma. But they were laughing at me and said Red was a bastard. I hit them as hard as I could. But there were too many of them."

Red's mother put the car in gear and said, "You know, I never much liked this town."

George smiled as he looked at his mother. "Me, either."

"Let's go get your brother and get out of this place."

The wind blew the paper map across Red's face. It and the dream startled him awake. He shook his head. The dream was real! His father had killed himself? It couldn't be true. Why wasn't he ever told? How many people really knew? All these years of unanswered questions crashed down like lightning splayed out in the darkness. A million clicking camera frames exploded into a horror movie playing out before his eyes.

What would bring a man, a father, a husband, to such a sad end? His father feeling worthless, unimportant, and so obsolete. He replayed his own life, his brain unable to process this new information. He analyzed it over and over again, never quite able to grasp it. He felt abandoned, cheated of life. His life was no longer about growing up, struggling to get ahead, striving to keep a family together without its father. But now, it was about his father's choice. A choice to leave a woman who'd loved him all her life. Abandoning two sons, leaving them to grow up without a father, and grandchildren without a grandfather.

It was still dark. Red gathered up camp. He checked his compass. East. He wanted his life back. He wanted it now.

CHAPTER 29

A s the afternoon passed, the sky clouded over with a wind that freshened from the south. Red roasted antelope meat over the fire and shared it with Jake and Lady. He watched a flight of geese overhead. Where were they going? Where was their home? What a view they must have, seeing places that he could never see. They were snow geese, handsome white birds with black wingtips. They wedged into the east. If only he could fly and see where they were leading.

He watched the embers float upward from the fire as drops of rain came down. He called Jake to the shelter, not out of concern but rather because he didn't want to smell a wet dog all night. It rained steadily but not hard. Red had always found the sound of the rain on the tarped lean-to to be magical and lulling. But not tonight. The thought of his father killing himself was too disturbing for him to sleep.

He was glad to have dry wood to pile on the fire toward morning. The rain quit as daylight came. The clouds were moving off, making it a good day for travel. Below in the grassland, the animals were back from wherever they had spent the night. The grass was wet with rain and bent over like it had bowed down but couldn't get up. Red knew the feeling. Thoughts of his brother remained in his mind. Why had George kept his father's death a secret?

It had been two months since George had left for Korea. Red's current purpose in life was to stop at the post office, go to school, and stop at the post office again. Each day, Red walked past a small house set back from the road and surrounded by large, overgrown maple trees. Each time, he'd see an old man sitting in a chair on the front porch. He wore the same clothing, had the same expression on his face, and was sometimes asleep and sometimes not. Red usually waved but got nothing in return.

It wasn't that Red felt sorry for the old man, but he thought they might have something in common: lonesomeness. He'd been tempted to speak to the man but, for some reason, never seemed to have the courage. But today would be different.

As he approached the front porch, Red said, "Hello."

An old Ford coupe was in the carport, covered in a layer of dust. The house was in need of repair but was definitely livable by minimum standards. There was no response from the old man. Red started to turn, to walk away and leave the man to himself. But Red had come this far, and it'd taken him weeks. He faced the man and cleared his throat. Red said hello again, but a bit louder this time.

The old man was startled and sat up with a question. "Salutations, who goes there?"

Salutations? What the heck does that mean? Red's voice quivered. He started again. "I'm Red Johnson. I live down the street."

The old man smiled. His wrinkled skin came to life. "How do you do, Mr. Johnson. Come on up here and let me get you a glass of iced tea."

Red stepped up to the porch. "My friends call me Red."

"Does that mean I'm your friend?"

Red didn't know what to say. Of course, they weren't friends. They hadn't even shaken hands. But they could be. By the time Red thought of a good response, the old man had gone into the house and returned with a mason jar full of iced tea.

Red drank the sweet tea and told the old man, "Thank you. It's just as good as my momma makes."

The old man's eyes were dull and empty. His skin was leaden and wrinkled and his voice raspy. His sporadic breaths between sentences gave way to pauses where he was seemingly searching for words. When he smiled, his teeth were few and yellowed. His hands were large and worn, and his fingernails were in need of trimming. Red had never before seen someone so old. How could someone get that many wrinkles and still be alive? The oldest person Red had ever talked to was Mr. Potter, a pig farmer who was probably not that old, really.

Red could tell the old man was at the age where life stopped offering and only took back. He wondered if the old man hurt. Red wanted to touch his skin, to see if it felt like a dead man's.

"I don't see too well anymore, but do they call you Red because of your hair?"

Red realized now why the old man had never waved back at him. "Yes, my brother started it."

The old man smiled.

Red told him all about George. Once he got going, he didn't stop.

It wasn't until several visits later that Red finally asked the old man for his name.

"My friends call me Custis."

"Does that mean we're friends?"

"Why, it certainly does."

Over the next few weeks, the two met just about every day after school. The old man would ask about homework and encouraged Red to complete it there on the front porch where he could offer help. Math seemed to be his specialty. They would trade stories, laugh, and sometimes just pass the time together saying nothing at all.

"I can still smell," Custis said.

"What?"

"You know that smell is the last of your senses to go? Your eyes go, then your hearing. Food tastes like it's all potatoes now. Potatoes with no salt or butter. And I can't remember the last time someone touched me."

Red stared at the old man.

"I'm still alive, though. I can still smell."

"Are you afraid to die?"

"Sometimes. Ever seen a dead person?"

"No. I ain't never felt one, either." A quiet pause lasted several seconds. "How do you think they feel? I mean, to touch?"

The old man held up his hand and spread his fingers as best as he could. "Put your hand up to mine."

Red placed his hand against the old man's hand.

"Take your other hand, your fingers, and feel our mirrored hands together. Now rub back and forth."

Red felt the mirrored fingers. "That's crazy! That feels crazy."

"I guess that's the closest I can come to describe the feeling."

"How old are you, Custis?"

"I'm old enough, I suppose. I've been waking up on this side of the grass for a long, long time. My nose and ears don't fit my head anymore. Seems that they're the only things that keep on growing. I used to think maybe my head was shrinking, but no, it's my nose and ears growing."

Each day, Red looked forward to seeing the old man, and each day, he shared stories of being with George. And on those special days when the mail brought letters from Korea, Red would read the letters aloud. Red wouldn't even open the envelopes until he reached the old man's house. Out of respect for Custis. The old man thought George was brave and noble and should run for president when he returned home. Red sometimes got three or four letters on the same day after a dry spell. Red would read the letters all in order and usually a second time through, just in case they'd missed something. The letters could never replace the time spent with his brother. But reading the letters made Red feel closer to him. The loneliness inside of Red had swallowed his heart whole.

Custis always listened with intensity. "You know what, Red? They say when you have mastered being alone, only then are you ready for the company of others. He'll be back soon, I just know it."

When they weren't talking about George, Red would listen to the old man's stories of his youth. Red tried to imagine a boy in the old man's face. Custis's voice turned velvety when he spoke of his younger years. "After you die, your soul returns to where it was the happiest. When I die, I'm going to Carolina." He paused and wiped his nose. "1901."

Custis closed his eyes and leaned his head back into the chair.

"I was thirty-six years old, and I had the world at my feet. I was in love with the prettiest girl in the world, and she was in love with me. She taught me to fly-fish, of all things. And I'm gonna get her back. That's the only thing that was ever worth a damn, 1901."

"What happened to her?"

"I made a mistake. I thought I was destined to change the world. I thought I was God's gift to society. I thought I was more important than anyone else. It was just before I left for New York."

Red loved to hear the old man's stories. He spoke about far-away places, like New York. And when Custis drifted off to nap, Red waited. There were no more weighty pauses in conversation but rather moments of stillness.

"I'm not much longer for this world. Strange thing about dying. We're all equal. No matter what you have or how important you are, how fancy your education is or how much money you have, we're all gonna die. Makes us all equal, so to speak. And nobody can talk their way or buy their way out of it. That's the one thing we all have in common. In the end, no one is more important than the man next to him."

Red thought about what the old man had just said. Death was a long way away for Red. It didn't apply to him. He was just a boy and had a lifetime ahead of him to figure things out. He looked at Custis. For the first time in weeks, Red saw the clouded eyes and wrinkles again. Age had abruptly returned. Red wished Custis could live forever. He wanted George to meet him.

"Oh, I suppose I made a difference. That's why I left in the first place, to make a difference in someone else's life. But I'm afraid the difference was made in mine." Tears welled in the old man's eyes.

Red let him remember.

The old man's voice was soft. He reconstructed the town. Red believed Custis had actually returned. He had to be there. He described every detail, who was standing on the corner, the storefronts, sounds, and even the smells. Custis retraced his steps down the sidewalk, holding hands with the most beautiful woman in the world.

"I try to go back as often as I can. I talk with my friends, walk down the streets, and swim in the lakes. There is no other place that I feel more alive than in that little town with my girl. I love her to this day."

It was getting colder in the mornings. Red worried about the old man not having winter clothing. Red's jackets wouldn't fit him, but he could borrow one of George's. Or he could bring him blankets and make sure he had enough firewood.

One morning, Red walked past the house on his way to school. The old man must have still been inside. After school was out, Red went back. A work truck was parked next to the porch, and a workman was boarding up the windows with a hammer and nails. Red hurriedly walked down the drive and asked the man what had happened.

"Not sure, just hired to board up the house."

The front door was closed. The chairs were missing from the front porch. Red tightened his lips and put his hands deep into his pockets. "Do you know if he died or something? Or moved? Did someone come and get him?"

"Like I said, I don't know. Everything should still be inside."

Red's heart rate was soaring. His voice rose an octave. "Can I go inside and take a quick look?"

The worker stopped hammering for a moment and said, "Not supposed to let anyone go in, but if you hurry, I don't reckon it will hurt."

Red realized for the first time that during the weeks he'd met with the old man, Custis had never left the porch. Red stepped inside. Custis had one chair, one glass, one fork, and one spoon. A stack of books stood in the corner of the living room.

In the bedroom, the bed was unmade and the blankets pulled back. The walls were adorned with photographs of a young man and woman dated *1901*. Some of the photographs were framed, some taped, and some attached with thumbtacks.

Beside the photographs were pages torn from magazines—various pictures of the countryside of the Carolinas. Most of the pages were black and white, with some newer ones in color. There were also a few articles marked with underlines and circles.

Three shirts were smartly hung in the closet next to one pair of pants. A pair of slippers was neatly placed on the floor beside the bed. A piece of paper protruded from between the mattress and box spring.

He lifted the top mattress, exposing three photo albums. He chose one and opened the cover. It contained a collection of newspaper articles, mainly from the *New York Times*, about Dr. Ronald Custis. The doctor had graduated with honors and was recognized around the world for his work with the mechanics of radiation and sound. He had been nominated for a Nobel Prize in 1924 and had retired in obscurity in 1925. A newspaper obituary was on the following page. *Heather Sarah Brannon, died 1925.* She was from a small town in North Carolina, had been married to the same man since 1902, and had four children, all girls. Her hobby was fly-fishing.

Custis was in Carolina now. He was in 1901 again.

Red hadn't thought of Custis in years. The memory was so fresh. Red wanted to talk with him, just one more time. He would love Addy. Matt and Sam, too. Together, they could wait for George again. Custis would have all the answers.

CHAPTER 30

Too many unanswered questions made the night long and restless. Red had been such a young, naïve soul back then. And Custis, a profoundly humbled and experienced man taught others contentment through his regret. Red wanted his life back. He wanted his youth. He wanted that little redheaded boy of fourteen years old to take the wisdom of Custis, the lessons of life learned far too late, and start over. He wouldn't work so hard. He'd let himself be happier and satisfied with what was laid out before him, enjoy what was in his hands. He would cherish friendships and nurture them even more. He'd take his Addy back to Vermont, her childhood home. They could ride the apple wagons in fall and the horse-driven sleighs in winter. They'd sip soft, warm cider from oversize mugs held in big, fluffy mittens. He would kiss her under the stars and watch the vapor of their breath between them. Above all, he would have the courage to speak from his heart, to say the words he felt to those he loved so deeply. He'd been a fool, a pride-filled fool.

The cold morning air forced Red from his bag. He started the fire, cooked his breakfast, and fed his dogs without using his left hand much. *Funny,* he thought, *you just don't know how much you use a muscle until it's damaged.* He changed the dressing on the swollen hand, added some ointment, and cleared camp. The dogs stayed close by as they romped ahead but still pretended to lead the way.

Sparse juniper and an occasional wind-stunted pine flecked the vast rolling prairies. The views were endless. With each crown of a hill, a new view of the prairie would appear and be just as breathtaking. Red daydreamed about the homesteads that had once filled the area. With each crest, he imagined seeing an old wooden barn with its prow jutting out, a weathered windmill slowly turning in the breeze, or scattered cattle fenced in with dilapidated wooden fence posts held up with rusty barbed wire.

His mind painted a canvas of discarded farm equipment left to corrode in a freshly plowed field. There off to the left, a field of manicured alfalfa furrows was lying in wait. Soon, there would be bales stacked high in the barn. And for a moment, he believed he could smell the freshly mown pasture wafting up the knoll. He prayed to be able to crown one more hill and see a ranch, busy with a herd of horses running freely with their fillies and colts in tow. But there was nothing except a 360-degree view of endless sky and boundless land. He stopped and tried to take it in. Without turning his head, he had a 180-degree view of distant thunderclouds dropping sweeping rain to the left and a contradicting cloudless blue sky on the right. Were he not looking at it with his own eyes, he would've called it impossible.

At night by the fire, he studied his maps. Laramie and Cheyenne would be his next destination. The air was cold, and the rain was heading his way. He watched the distant lightning and listened to the tailing thunder. The small, lightweight tent was big enough for both him and Jake, if neither one moved too much. Each morning, Lady would appear in the distance and then playfully reunite with her family. The smell of fresh rain on dusty prairie grass and sage was intoxicating.

What was it about the first fall rain? Red wondered. Was it the magic of changing seasons, the promise of never-ending life?

Red had forgotten about his injured thumb. The pain was gone, and so was the tenderness. He removed the bandage, expecting to find seeping blood from an ill-aligned muscle, red with infection. But he found nothing. The wound had completely healed. He examined his hand and moved his thumb back and forth. He cut away the sutures. Not even a scar!

He must've miscalculated the days. No, he must have hallucinated. Red picked up the discarded bandages. The dried blood was proof it had happened. He held his hand closer to the fire's light. He was losing his mind again. Drifting into madness, psychosis consuming brain cells while regenerating others in his hand. "No! Stop it! I'm not gonna let this happen. I just lost track of the days."

Red sat down. He forced breath in and out through his clenched teeth, spewing spit with each exhale. Red held his journal close to the fire. *What day is it?* No entries for the last thirteen days. How could he have forgotten? Red fought inside his mind. He had to be in control. Red rocked back and forth telling himself, "OK, OK. I'm thirteen days ahead."

It was hard for him to fall asleep. His mind was busy and wouldn't stop churning. Random thoughts burst into his head, all garbled together, unable to follow any logical thread. Fear followed him into sleep until he was awakened by Jake's growls. He grabbed for his shotgun and opened the small tent flap. The fire was dim but was still going. Red threw sage on the fire, and it immediately lit up the night with flames and rising embers.

Jake paced back and forth and barked into the darkness. A screeching cry sounded in the distance. It was from a mountain lion circling the camp but keeping its distance. Red loaded the fire with wood and more sage. He wrapped himself in the sleeping bag and sat by the fire with Stubs across his lap for the rest of the night. The red coals deep in the fire were hypnotic. Red couldn't take his eyes off of the fire as he thought of his life. He missed simplicity. He missed growing up with his brother. He missed his family and missed his old life. He asked God to protect his Lady from the lion and let his mind return to thoughts of his past.

He was happy to have gotten out of school. Red hated to be indoors. It meant confinement, being controlled by other people, and obligations he did not wish to have. He carried his books home but knew he wouldn't open them until Monday morning. As he hurried toward home, he'd planned on getting his .22 rifle to go squirrel shooting. His mother would still be asleep after working the night shift at the local ten-bed hospital. If he were quiet enough, she'd never know.

There were two cars parked in front of his house. Who was about to ruin his chances of going shooting? Now his mother was surely awake. As he came closer, Red stopped in the middle of the road. His books fell to the ground while his hasty walk turned into slow, deliberate steps. He heard his mother screaming inside the house. He recognized Pastor Hayes's old car, which displayed a decal of a purple cross in the front corner of the windshield. The other car was dark and shiny. An army insignia was painted on the door. The same insignia that had been on George's letters, sent from places Red couldn't pronounce.

Red walked onto the front porch. His chest tightened with each step. Clenched fists remained at his side. He wanted to pull them up in front of him, protect himself from what might be. The wood floor creaked beneath his feet. The front door was open. Red looked through the screen door. His mother was sitting on the couch. Two dark figures stood over her. Two officers with caps tucked under their arms. Pastor Hayes stood, head down toward his chest. His mother's face was empty of life.

"We don't know exactly what happened," a deep voice stated. "His entire company was lost. We do know that they knocked out a high-priority enemy position." The silence was sinister, sucking oxygen from the air. "Ma'am, please know that what your boy was part of saved hundreds, maybe thousands, of our men."

His mother looked straight forward. Her voice was dry and resolute. "Don't you dare try to tell me he was a hero. He was a hero long before the army ever got him. You don't know anything about my son! You don't even know what happened to him."

"The United States military will be eternally grateful for your sacrifice."

She slowly stood, hands down at her sides. "Now, get out of my house."

Red turned, bolting off the porch. He ran past his books, which lay in an abandoned pile in the middle of the roadway. He ran down the street and turned into the woods. It didn't matter what direction, he just ran as fast as he could.

George had lied. He'd lied about leaving. He'd lied about always being there. He'd lied about coming home. George was a liar. He had lied about everything. Red's eyes focused only forward. He wasn't scared of what lay ahead but rather what was behind. His arms pumped, front to back, trying to help his body go faster. Distance was all that mattered. To be detached from the truth. George was dead. His promise was broken. Brush and tree limbs tore into his skin. His flimsy summer clothing ripped easily. He ran like crashing waves that didn't care what they could destroy. He was unstoppable. He dare not turn his head. He was winning the race. His lungs burned for air, and his leg muscles were numb with adrenaline as his heart tried to claw its way out of his chest. A log was just ahead, but he didn't see it. Face-first, he skid to the forest floor. He felt the coolness of the duff, or maybe blood. Momentum drove him farther along the ground. Back to his feet, without turning, he continued. Distance. All he needed was distance.

He didn't know how long, or even how many days, he stayed there in the woods. When he returned home, his mother met him at the front door.

"I know you heard, Red. I knew you'd be OK." His mother opened the screen, grabbed her son tightly, and both cried together.

Pastor Hayes and close friends came by regularly over the next two weeks. George's body finally came home. Red was fourteen years old, nearly fifteen. He insisted on driving his mother the two hundred miles back to their small hometown where George would be buried next to his father.

"Momma, it's my job now. George would want me to take care of you."

His mother smiled. "I know."

The roads and towns they passed along the way were unfamiliar to Red. His mother was quiet and solemn. At times, her stare hesitated, sometimes on a storefront or a farmhouse. Red knew things and places must have been significant to her. She was lost in her memories. He just wanted it to be over.

George was buried next to his father. A soldier handed his mother a folded flag, then whispered something to her. She politely smiled.

After everyone had walked away, Red placed his fishing pole on top of the casket. Red wanted to tell George that he would need the pole now. He could fish while waiting for Red to someday join him. He'd need the head start. Red's words were stuck in his throat. He wanted to speak, he had so much to say. So many unanswered questions and emotions never addressed. *It's not really happening, but the coffin is there.* He could see it. George said he'd come back. But not like this. They had so much more to do. They were best friends, and best friends didn't lie.

This would be his last memory of his brother. A brother once full of passion and warmth now lying in pieces in a cold wooden box, being covered up with dirt. It wasn't fair. He wanted the image out of his head.

Red didn't know what to do. He didn't want to leave his brother in the ground all alone. He wanted to crawl in there with him. They could be together again. He heard his mother's voice in the distance.

"Red. He's going to be fine now. He's with his daddy."

The words trembled out: "Goodbye, George."

The broken boy walked down the hill and watched an older man approach his mother. He was thin. He looked kind. The old man removed his hat and held it down in front of him. He nervously rolled the brim with both hands as he spoke. Red could barely hear what was being said. His mother must have known the man. She leaned into him, hugged him, and patted his back. The old man looked embarrassed, maybe. He wiped his eyes with a handkerchief removed from his vest pocket. His mother seemed to be reassuring him, both nodding their heads as if agreeing to something.

The old man spoke softly. "You should have taken my money. I lost you for so long. Then you moved again and again."

"It meant the world to me that you cared so much, but I just couldn't take it."

"But I promised your husband." Their conversation stopped as Red approached.

"This is my son Red. This is Mr. Sandersson. He knew your daddy a long time ago."

Mr. Sandersson reached out and shook Red's hand. The handshake lingered. Mr. Sandersson acted like he was at a loss for words. Red let the man gather himself. "Your father was good man. And George. He was good boy, too. You come from good people, son." He spoke carefully, and with an accent. *It must be foreign,* Red thought. Red was confused. He didn't know whether it was because of the accent or if there was actually something familiar about the man. "You are so tall. You look like your poppa."

Two days after the funeral, a letter arrived in the mail. It was from George. It'd taken six weeks to be delivered from Korea. Twenty-four years would pass before Red's mother could unseal and read it. She shared it with her grown son. George's handwriting was neat and perfect as always. He wrote about the weather, the landscape, and the fish. He wrote about the people and their sadness and about his company and their bravery. He wrote about lying down at night and looking up at the stars and knowing that Red would be looking up at the very same stars in just a few short hours.

Tell my Pollux I caught the biggest and ugliest fish I ever set my eyes on. He ended the letter with: *I love you, Momma, and I'll see you soon. I'll be back before you can miss me. Always, your son, George.*

It made her smile. Red's mother died in her sleep that very night. Red never truly understood his mother's pain. She had been more worried about Red's heartache than her own. She was fiercely protective until the day she left the earth. Red had been thirty-eight years old. Old enough to have figured his life out. It must've been time for his mother to be with George again.

Everything the boy in his memory and the old man now sitting alone had achieved was now lost. He had wasted so much time. He had left his mother when she'd needed him most. He should have taken care of her rather than running away for days like a selfish child throwing a fit. She had raised two boys without their father and managed a household on her own. Her burdens had been deep, scarring her for life. Red should have helped more. That was his job. He'd owed that to his mother, to George, and to himself.

Red couldn't hold in his tears. The fire had long since died, the sun had been up for hours, but Red was still wrapped up in the sleeping bag, sitting next to Jake. Lady returned safely to camp and lay down quietly beside her family.

CHAPTER 31

T hey'd never known what had happened to George, other than
that his entire task force was lost. Red walked for miles. Travel
seemed slow. He didn't eat and only drank when he saw that
his dogs were thirsty. The sun was in the western sky. Almost a full
day, lost in thought. How many miles had he been able to cover? Red
checked the compass. At least he was still on course. He no longer felt
the weight of the backpack or the pain in his legs. He was numb, his
muscles on autopilot. He wanted his mind to do the same, to think
about superficial fodder. But all thoughts led him back to his mother.

The cemetery was overgrown and littered with dry leaves and
undergrowth beneath a tall canopy of oak trees. It was protected by an
unkempt wrought-iron fence. The grave markers designated old family
plots, some with ornate, lichen-masked monuments and others with

just an ordinary meek stone waning in time. Red stood in front of his father's headstone. To one side lay George's headstone. To the other side, his mother's dirt-covered grave.

Red's voice quavered with emotion, her death still fresh in his heart. "I took care of her the best I could, Daddy. Now it's your turn. She never loved anyone else but you. She loved George and me, but, I mean, she just loved you her whole life. She likes to sit and read in the early morning with her coffee, in the quiet, before anyone else is awake, OK?"

Red looked away, then back down at the gravestones.

"She loves the smell of the first September rain. And children, she loves children, the sound of laughter. And she loves lavender, the smell, the color—just lavender. But you know that. I always tried to hold her hand, too, no matter how old I got. I always held on to her."

He knelt down and ran his fingers across every letter in his father's name. *George Johnson, Sr. 1903 to 1941, 38 yrs.*

"She always told me, 'Nothing is ever written in stone,'" he said, trying to muster a smile. He stood without taking his eyes off of the engraved letters. The wind softly blew as he looked up to the sky. A tear trickled down to the corner of his mouth.

"She has you and George now, so I know she'll be so happy. I know she'll be safe." He looked at his mother's marker. *Rebecca M. Johnson. 1913 to 1975, 62 yrs.* Then to his brother's headstone. *George Johnson, Jr. 1933 to 1952, 19 yrs. My brother was the keeper of my heart.*

He placed a copper penny on top of his brother's headstone. It was shiny next to five others that had turned dark with patina. Red wiped the tears from his face with the back of his hand. His father had not lived long enough to see his sons grow. His brother was robbed of his full life, and his mother had lived years pining for both of them. Red was a foundling, the sole survivor of his generation. He sniffed his runny nose, walked to his car, and drove away.

Red was on the front side of the Rocky Mountains. He'd crossed over the Continental Divide, a feat that even he was amazed by. He looked at the massive snow-covered mountain range that filled the distant horizon. His long, arduous travel into Idaho and over into Wyoming had been the right choice. He was alive.

The plains were blown barren by the season's wind and rain. Prairie channels meandered throughout the grassland knolls and were sometimes dotted with scattered cottonwood and oak. It was there the trees imparted their secreted water source.

The prairies were now sporadically infused with large rock outcroppings and the occasional monolithic rock, jutting up as if it should be on the rugged Oregon coast. The rocky cliffs harbored bighorn sheep. It would be their hides that would protect Red during the winter.

He picked up Lone Tree Creek, which would lead over a hundred miles directly south to the South Platte River, where Greeley used to be. From there, it would be sixty-five miles to Denver. His winter cave would be due south, another seventy-five miles to Manitou Springs.

Red was so close. If he made it to the cave, he would survive for sure. Crossing the Rockies had seemed nearly impossible. But he'd made it against all odds. But, now, winter was setting in. The prairies were easy walking but provided no shelter. If anything delayed him now, he would die. The cave was within reach, if only the weather would hold.

It was midday before Red stopped to rest. He dropped his pack, guns, and other equipment to the ground but continued to walk for several hundred feet. He stopped, fell to his knees, and cried. Red didn't know whether it was exhaustion, altitude sickness, or just him going crazy. Jake sat down next to him with Lady watching from a distance. Red grabbed the dog and sobbed until he was emotionally spent. By evening, he returned to his pack and equipment, made camp in the middle of the prairie, and tried to sleep.

Red lay inside his tent. The last of the firelight cast odd shadows on the side. The nylon material fluttered with the wind. It was a flag, a single flag on a dark prairie no one would ever see. His mind was filled with memories of his childhood. His mother had never been the same after George's death. She'd taken responsibility for allowing him to go. Red could always see it in her eyes—an emptiness he could never quite fill. She died without knowing what had actually happened. Maybe it was better that way. Red fell asleep and dreamt of George.

Rocks and boulders protruded through a light layer of snow. Winter's trees stood silent with clinging patches of frozen white outlining their branches and twigs. Muddy tire ruts led the six-man unit through the desolate winter landscape. The battlefield lay quiet except for the slosh of muddy snow under-boot. Their faces dirty, each impassively staring in different directions, men who were once boys. The army-issued snow ponchos concealed their heavy packs. George's drab-green metal helmet was marred with scratches and speckled with undercoats of gray and splotches of chipped white paint. His blue eyes were the only thing of color in the underworld of black, gray, and white. His face focused, barely old enough to need to shave.

The leader stopped and gave a hand signal, his gaze resolute. His fisted hand came up quickly. The unit stopped just as fast. A tank. The rumble in the ground always came before the sound. They knew its consequence well. The leader motioned to his men to take cover, and they did so without pause. The men left the open roadway and ran deeper into the woods. They stood quiet and motionless as a convoy of enemy tanks and trucks passed by.

"You think they just came from the bridge, sir?" one of the men asked.

"No doubt. It must be close by," the leader responded.

The men tucked their faces into their chests to conceal the vapor of their breaths. The vibration of the passing machinery quivered the ground. There they remained until nothing could be heard or felt.

It began to snow softly as the men advanced up a small ridge. Upon reaching the rim, the men lay on their bellies to look down at the valley below, some using binoculars. An entire convoy of Korean tanks, trucks, and equipment moved on both sides of a river. Two platoons or more shuffled below like a city plopped down randomly in a barren and marred land.

"There it is," the lieutenant whispered. "How many you got, Gonzales?"

"I'm still counting. At least a hundred seventy-five, along with five tanks. Six. Thirty-five trucks. I can't tell what they're doing."

A wide, muddy river wove back and forth through the valley, forming oxbows that once must've been fields bountiful with crops. But no bridge crossed the deep, fast-flowing water.

George whispered jokingly, "Look at those trucks headed for the river. They're just gonna drive right on top of the water."

And they did.

The trucks and equipment lined up on the far side of the water-course. One by one, they drove into the water but did not sink more than a couple of inches.

George quietly sighed. "That water's thirty feet deep!"

Another voice whispered, "If that's Jesus driving, we're on the wrong side."

The water was brown, showing nothing beneath its surface. A tank reached the other side. A large utility truck followed.

"It's a water bridge," one of the men whispered.

One by one, the vehicles crossed as if the water were an illusion.

"I'll be damned," the lieutenant said. "They built a bridge right beneath the surface. All this time, it's been right there. No wonder air support missed it."

Another whisper. "Damn, I bet that's how they've been disappearing into thin air."

George removed scope equipment from his pack and obtained the coordinates of the bridge. George was in his element, but his hands still trembled. He doubled-checked just in case. The numbers were the same. The others watched with intensity. The magnitude of the situation was setting in.

"Hurry up, Johnson. What are you doing, eating your lunch?"

George didn't break concentration. "Shut up."

George relayed the final numbers and secured his scopes back to his field pack. The squad retreated down the ridge and back into the woods. The communications officer tried to radio for support but was unable to muster more than white noise. Again, the coordinates were relayed. A garbled voice confirmed some of the numbers.

"Did they get it?"

"I think so, Lieutenant."

"OK, let's move back up there. We'll have better communications."

The squad returned to the edge of the woods and began to ascend the ridge. The lieutenant abruptly stopped. He stood motionless, his face rigid with fear. He slowly looked down at his feet and, as softly as he could, said, "Son of a bitch, I stepped on a mine. I heard it click."

George was closest and took a step toward the lieutenant.

The lieutenant ordered George and the rest of the men to back out. George didn't move. He looked at the other men and whispered, "Back out now. Step in your own tracks." George knelt down on his knees in front of the lieutenant. He brushed the light layer of snow from around the bottom of the lieutenant's boot with his partially gloved hands, exposing a circular metal disc.

"Don't move, LT," George whispered.

"No shit!"

The lieutenant relinquished his command and ordered George to get back with the unit. George stared at the land mine, his mind searching, replaying, and strategizing. He wiped the sweat from his eyes with the back of his hand. It had only been seconds, but in his mind, it felt like it had been hours.

"Johnson!" It was as loud as the lieutenant could speak without breaking a whisper.

George looked up at a panicked face. He'd never realized the lieutenant had red hair. He could tell by the stubble on his face.

"You're the specialist, Johnson. The river should be within a half mile. You've got the coordinates."

George leaned his upper body back away from the lieutenant's feet. He looked at the other men standing stationary, now about fifty yards away. George saw their chests rising with quick, shallow breaths, which matched their beating hearts.

George quickly unlaced and removed his left boot and placed it on the snow beside him. An angry whisper followed: "What the hell are you doing, Johnson? I ordered you back to the unit—now. If this goes off, the bridge remains, and we'll all be dead within five minutes."

George removed what was left of his glove. He rubbed his hands together, held them to his mouth. He warmed his fingers with his breath. "What is your name?"

"I'm ordering you to continue—take out that bridge."

"Sir, with all due respect, you're not in a position to negotiate. What is your name?"

The lieutenant stuttered. "MacPhail."

"No, I mean your first name. What's your first name?"

"Kevin. Kevin MacPhail." He paused. "Well, that's my middle name. My first is Elmore."

"Yeah. Kevin's better."

George removed the large knife from his belt. He placed the tip of the knife under the bottom lace of the lieutenant's boot. He sliced all the laces in half. The boot was muddy and tattered. Tape had been wrapped around the toe area to keep the sole from separating from the leather. George pulled the filleted boot front open. The green sock was wet. His foot must have been so cold, George thought.

As George cut away at the edge of the tape, the lieutenant said, "Johnson, if this goes off, we won't have a chance of taking it out again. No one knows about it except us." The lieutenant told George that he would stay on the mine until he could hear them taking out the bridge. "Besides, I'll wait until you get back. It's only gonna take off my leg, and you sorry bastards will just have to carry me all the way back. Might do me some good to have the rest anyway."

George's knife was sharp. It sliced through the tape on the front of the boot. The sole was already partially detached from the leather top, and it was easy for the knife to sever the remaining leather.

George leaned back and rested on his legs. He nervously rubbed his mouth with his hands as if to borrow time. He didn't have time to think about getting hurt. Dying was not in the equation. He had spontaneously acted out of need, for another human being, another soul who had the responsibility to guide six other boys safely back to their families.

The lieutenant was still giving orders, but George was oblivious. He looked up at the lieutenant and then over to one of the men.

George softly shouted, "Give me your spade."

The soldier didn't move, and again, George demanded the shovel. One of the other men moved forward, deliberately stepping in the boot tracks already in the snow.

When the soldier was close enough to safely toss the shovel to George, he said, "Here, take mine."

George motioned for him to throw it and caught it with his right hand. His eyes met with the frightened eyes of the young soldier. "It'll be OK. The LT will get you home." George smiled, but the boy could not. George pushed down with pressure across the top of the boot with his left hand and with the other carefully worked the spade head back and forth between the sole of the boot and the lieutenant's foot.

The lieutenant gritted his teeth and said, "You stabbed my foot—now I'm gonna die of tetanus. I don't mean to be ungrateful or anything, but if I have to die, I want to go quick."

George adjusted the spade and, in one motion, shoved the blade under the lieutenant's foot and out the other side of the boot. All in one motion, George placed his weight on either side of the spade.

"Pull your foot out, sir."

"Johnson, what are you doing?" the lieutenant demanded.

"Five against a hundred and fifty." George made sure the others could not hear. "We're outnumbered, and we're all probably gonna die, anyway. You need to lead. That's your job. Go get the bridge, sir."

The lieutenant ordered George to take command of the unit.

"No, sir, it's your unit. I'll die here right with you if you don't take your damn stinking foot out of this boot right now."

The lieutenant didn't move.

"If this goes off, it'll kill us both, then your remaining men got a hundred of them comin' over that hill. They won't have a chance."

The lieutenant slowly removed his foot from the filleted boot. George increased the downward pressure. The lieutenant picked up George's boot from the snow and stepped away.

"Why you, Johnson?" asked the lieutenant.

George continued pushing on the spade with both hands and did not look up. George didn't want him to see the tears in his eyes. He didn't want that to be the last view the lieutenant had of him. George wiped his eyes against his shoulder, hoping to disguise it as rubbing the sweat away.

"Well, I guess I'm the only one here with a size thirteen shoe, you big oaf." George finally looked up at the lieutenant. "Go get them, Kevin, and by the time you come back for me, I'll have this all figured out."

No other words were said. None were needed. As the men departed, they turned their heads away, hiding their eyes.

Red was restless but still deep in his dream. Jake lay close by and watched his master.

George's hands had gone numb and colorless. He'd lost track of time after the first hour. Distant explosions erupted from the ridge. He hoped it was the bridge being blown to pieces. The sound of muffled gunfire followed. It must have been a thousand bursts. He wanted to look toward the heavens but couldn't move his head.

The snow continued, and what little definition there had been between gray and white diminished even further. George was sure hypothermia had set in. His mind was convoluted with thoughts and memories. Indiscernible voices approached as uniformed Koreans surrounded George. The metal disk and spade were now just below a blanket of white. His helmet was covered with a thick layer of icy snow. His face was almost colorless, except for his bluish lips. His eyelashes were dusted with frost, his pupils almost white. He was blind now and shook involuntarily. It was all he could do to keep the spade in its place.

He moved his head toward the enemy and managed a few broken syllables: "I'm hurt—I give up, I surrender. Surrender."

A Korean motioned with his rifle to another to go toward George. A soldier gestured to George to stand but got no response. The commander yelled at the soldier, then the soldier yelled at George.

"I surrender, surrender," George said.

The soldiers kept their rifles pointed directly at George, too afraid to step any closer. The leader was clearly frustrated with his men's cowardice. He bolted past his soldiers, pushing them out of his way. The officer stepped toward George and leaned down to look at him. Two more soldiers approached cautiously.

"Hurt bad, surrender, surrender."

The leader held his rifle at the ready and advanced until he stood directly in front of George. The barrel end of the long rifle was placed on the front of George's helmet. George felt the click of the two metals colliding. He couldn't see what it was. He waited. Another click. Three more pokes to his shoulders and back. There must be three soldiers within reach, all prodding him with their rifles now. George looked up with his frozen, colorless eyes and, in that last moment, stopped shaking before he calmly leaned back. He pulled his frozen hands and shovel out from beneath the snow.

CHAPTER 32

The sound of the explosion woke Red in horror. The dream was real. He held on to his chest as if trying to stop himself from gasping. Red was sweating. He tasted vomit in his mouth. Adrenaline kept him from fainting. His mind flashed back to the front porch of his home. The two officers telling his mother that George was dead. "The entire unit was lost." That George was killed trying to save his team. The dream was real. It had to be real. His mind couldn't have concocted such specific detail. The dream had been comprehensive and precise.

The air was thin and black. He needed oxygen. He needed out of the tent. Red crawled over Jake and grabbed at the tent zipper. He pulled, tugged, but nothing happened. He couldn't see. His fingers searched, groping for the tab. He opened his eyes wide but could see nothing. He couldn't breathe, the air was gone. He had to flee—there was nothing to fight. He crawled back to the top of the sleeping bag and fumbled for his knife. He plunged the knife blade into the side of the tent, the middle of where the flag had been. The blade ripped the material straight to the ground.

A soft layer of snow covered the ground. The same snow that was in his dream, but without blood and broken bodies. The fire was nearly out. He stirred the last of the embers and added some wood. He called Jake to his side and covered their shoulders with the sleeping bag. After all these years, did he finally know the truth? Why was this happening now? Red pulled his knees to his chest and wrapped his arms around his shins. Red buried his face downward into his chest.

Courage, the sum total of all virtue, with humility at its center, had been displayed in a single moment halfway around the world. That's how George had always been. He'd died revealing the truest form of agape love, and Red had hated him in return. How self-absorbed Red had been. Red wanted to go to hell.

The truth needed to be buried in a grave deep beneath the grass where no one would ever find it. All these years, he had hated his brother for leaving him. He'd hated him for dying. He'd hated George for killing part of his mother's heart, something impossible to repair. Red had thought George had abandoned his family, left them all alone, discarded them like surplus property. Just like their father. That was the narrative Red had harbored deep inside. But now that he knew the truth, how could he forgive himself?

Hours passed before Red was able to collect himself. He broke camp and continued south. The sun brought warmth, and the light dusting of snow slowly disappeared.

He stopped near a large rock monolith. He recognized the rock formation from photographs. It looked like a castle, a fortress far above, safe from society. The climb to the top would be difficult. It just might kill him.

Red clambered to the top of the monolith, leaving the dogs far below. He stood at the top and placed the tips of his boots over the edge. He closed his eyes and breathed in deeply. He slowly began to recite various quotes and poems with perfect execution. With the talent of the most versatile thespian, Red morphed into each character.

"'To be, or not to be, that is the question: Whether 'tis nobler in the mind to suffer the slings and arrows of outrageous fortune, or to take arms against a sea of troubles . . . call me Ishmael; some years ago—never mind how long precisely—having little or no money in my purse, and nothing particular to interest me on shore, I thought I would sail about a little and see the watery part of the world . . . And so, my fellow Americans: ask not what your country can do for you—ask what you can do for your country . . . And therefore never send to know for whom the bell tolls; it tolls for thee.'

"'I could have been a contender . . . Say hello to my little friend . . . Frankly, my dear, I don't give a damn . . . Anyone can be president, that's the problem . . . Night Grandpa, night Elizabeth, night John-boy . . . Nobody puts baby in the corner . . . I see dead people . . . I'll be back . . . ET, phone home . . . Talk to me, Goose . . . To the moon, Alice, to the moon . . . I'm an excellent driver, yeah . . . If I only had a brain . . . Put 'em up, put 'em up . . . And your little dog, too . . . There's no place like home, there's no place like home . . . I'm your huckleberry . . . I gotta find Bubba . . . Lieutenant Dan, I got you some ice cream . . .'

"'Do you like green eggs and ham—I do not like them, Sam-I-am. I do not like green eggs and ham . . . Bueller, anyone, Bueller? . . . Rapunzel, Rapunzel, let down your hair . . . What is it you want, Mary, what do you want, you want the moon, just say the word and I'll throw a lasso around it and pull it down . . . Wilson! . . . Houston, we have a problem . . .'"

Red paused as he had run out of breath. His speech was broken, but he fought to stay conscious.

"'Scotty, beam me up. Just beam me up.'"

Red collapsed to the ground.

He was awakened by the dog licking his face. Groggy and confused, he could hear Jake barking incessantly far below but was unable to figure out how he was licking his face until he realized it was Lady. How she'd been able to climb with only three legs, he didn't know. He shook his head and tried to force some sense back into it. It was late afternoon, and he figured he must've been out for hours.

He stood and looked westward. The land before him was layered with miles of open golden prairie backed by rolling hills of light-green sage, which progressed into purple mountains acting as ramparts to the snow-covered crags and peaks of the Rocky Mountains. Pikes Peak stood sentinel over the entire land. Herds of roaming buffalo flecked the majestic prairie before him. It took him about an hour to carefully descend the monolith. Lady had passed him and was waiting at the bottom with Jake.

Red was exhausted, but clarity was slowing returning. It was so easy to fall into desperation, to give up, to take the coward's way out. He could die peacefully and end all his pain. But that dream of George . . . George had the strength of angels, and now, Red had to go on. Red was finally learning things he had ached for most of his life. He was getting answers but needed more. *What caused my father to kill himself? Where did everyone go?* He had to stay lucid and fight until he had his family back.

Red returned to his equipment and tried to gather his wits. For the next two days, he camped in the same spot. He rested, repaired his tent, and made sure he ate well. He believed he was within fifty miles of the cave.

The terrain was easy, almost flat. A light breeze kept him chilly. He came to a rise in the land, a small grass-covered knoll in the middle of the prairie. All that was visible for miles was the moody sky, sprinkles of grazing deer far off in the distance, Jake's raised tail bobbing in the tall grass, and the outlying range of the Rocky Mountains. He crested the knoll, stopped, and gave thanks for the gift of such splendor. The waist-high grass stood rank and file. He moved with opened arms, as if he were a pawn in a life-size chess game. Everything was alive in this world, bonded with familial spirit but ruled by a natural world hierarchy.

He pushed down the grasses and made a flat area in which to lie down. The grass fortress shielded him from the brisk wind and allowed the sun to reach him without interruption. The sudden warmth of the harbor was mesmerizing as it invited him down. Red removed his clothing and set it aside. He lay on his back with his arms stretched outward. He felt the sun penetrate his skin and soak into his body. A moving, warm radiance of contentment. He wanted his body to be regenerated, his mind to heal. He wanted his heart to forgive itself for harboring unjust emotions.

For just a little while, Red allowed himself to be open. He was free of restraints. Free of displaced anger, burdens, and even fear. He looked at the soft white clouds moving in the blue sky above and thought of his Addy. He remembered the first time he'd seen her. It was a warm summer's day a long time ago.

Red was a married man but sat alone near the back of the church. He came early and had carefully picked out an empty pew toward the back, away from the center aisle, as inconspicuous as possible. It had been years since he had attended. He read through the service program and fidgeted in his seat. Familiar names brought a smile to his face. He hadn't seen them in years. He browsed through the hymnal and grinned as he found some of the same old verses he had sung as a small boy with his mother in a church far away. He felt a familiar comfort. His tanned skin and deep-red hair accentuated the whiteness of his shirt, and the blue in his loosened tie matched his eyes.

He watched the people walk down the center aisle as they entered through the double church door behind him. There were children, some unruly, some not; couples holding hands and chatting, and some not; old ladies smiling and laughing, and some not. He looked back down at the hymnal and thought of his marriage. A soft sound of laughter brought his eyes up to the center of the aisle to the side of him.

A woman was shaking hands with an elderly couple. She used both of her hands. She held the grasp, delaying a bit before letting go. She must have wanted them to know how much she cared. She was genuine, and whatever the conversation was, she was nothing but sincere and authentic. He could see her eyes, a penetrating blue. Her brown hair was softly pulled upward, away from her face. He imagined that, had she not been in church, it would've hung carefree. The woman sat down near the front of the church, then disappeared into the congregation.

While the rest of the assembly sang aloud, Red enjoyed silently reading along. Page 299, "Morning Has Broken." Of all the songs, that had been one of Red's favorites. The sermon was good. Red stood, hoping for a quick exit, but was delayed by loitering congregants. He watched the woman he'd noticed earlier pass by. He wanted to avert his eyes, hide his stare, but could only manage to shift his head downward. He watched, and for a moment, he thought their eyes met. She was holding the hand of a small girl. The girl must have been three, maybe four. Red couldn't hear what the woman said to others as she moved toward the exit, but it was obvious she cherished the child. He wanted to meet the woman. He wanted to know everything about her. She was simply beautiful all the way through. Just for a moment, it was hard for him to breathe. He wanted to shout out to her, capture her attention. She was walking by, leaving the church. His chance would be gone in only a moment. Red took a step toward her. He couldn't move his other foot.

Red felt Jake lay down beside him. He reached out and touched Jake's warm, thick coat and told him he was a good dog. He wanted to remember more about Addy and thought about all the days that had been spent away from her. So much time wasted apart. What had happened to the rainy days spent together in bed, reading stories aloud to one another?

Addy finished the last page, the epilogue of *Doctor Zhivago*. "Did you like it?"

"Honey, your voice inflection could stir a mule into promiscuity."

Addy laughed. "OK, Red, it's your turn."

Red opened his book. He tugged at the comforter and snuggled Addy in closer. He attempted to imitate his wife's ability to capture each nuance in the writing. In a hushed voice, he began, "The stock is fully inletted but requires some additional cutting to get the proper depth for the tang, lock, side plate, and trigger guard. These parts . . ."

Lady yapped in the distance. Red snapped back to the present and quickly sat up. Lady stood in the grass on the next knoll, looking directly at him. Her long variegated brown-and-golden coat moved in concert with the dried windblown grasses. It was time to go.

CHAPTER 33

It took him two days to reach the area known as Garden of the Gods.
It was more spectacular than he'd imagined. Red had seen the
imposing statues of sedimentary rock for the last thirty miles. The
closer he got, the grander the spires became. Out of thin soil and surrounded by low-growing green-gray shrubs of spiky yucca, the imposing families of red rock jutted hundreds of feet into the air. They were
ambassadors from another time and looked like a computer-generated
backdrop on a movie set. The coral-salmon color of the stone was mar-
velously in utter contrast with the blue sky above and the green sage
and scrub pines at its base.

He could not recall exactly why this place had been named Garden
of the Gods, but he could imagine. This hallowed land was not only a
mosaic of color but a montage of the territories that Red had walked

over the last year. It was the earth's gathering place: the plains of dry prairie grasslands, the foothills of shrubs and scrubby trees, the thick montane evergreen forests, and the alpine tundra of the snowcapped Rocky Mountains. It was like the four corners of the earth all met together in the Garden of the Gods. Maybe that was the origin of the name. Other than holding his newborn infant son in his arms for the first time, Red had never felt so close to God.

The Garden of the Gods somehow reassured him all was right and this was the place he needed to be. He scouted the area for shelter but continued to be distracted at the beauty before him. He stood at the base of sheer red cliffs that rose hundreds of feet toward the heavens. From a distance, he studied the once-horizontal layered sediments, now tilted mountains in kaleidoscope colors. Solitary twisted juniper trees, shaped by the winds, grew straight out of the hard rock crevasses, barely tethered to the earth. Colonies of birds nested and played in the nooks and crannies of the spires. He could see bighorn sheep atop a large, craggy rock formation and small herds of pronghorn grazing in the distance. •

He made camp at the base of one of the cliffs where he would be protected on three sides from nighttime intruders. Over the next several days, depending on the weather, he planned to explore the area and attempt to find the Cave of the Winds nearby.

The night air was cold and black. Light from the campfire reflected off the red cliff rocks and created a flickering movement that encompassed the camp. Howls of coyotes breached the quiet night. Lady stayed close to camp and did not venture out of sight. Morning came with thunderclouds and the biggest drops of rain Red had ever seen or felt. The contrast of dark clouds above brilliant-red rocks was impossibly stunning. He threw the tarp over his belongings, skipped breakfast in his excitement, and set off to explore the area. He had traveled nearly halfway across the United States. And survived. His excitement energized his mind. He had accomplished the impossible.

Massive clouds came from the west and seemed to collide with the mountain peaks. Rain and hail pounded the ground in short bursts, then gave way to patches of bright-blue sky and rays of sun. Rainwater formed small streams that ran swiftly through the thin veneer of soil, exposing the solid rock just beneath.

He accidently scared up a mule deer then watched it stot through spiky yuccas, squat pines, and junipers. Red's excitement in seeing a big buck never seemed to diminish. They were proud and graceful animals that demanded respect, if only for their beauty. Their stateliness still took his breath away. He'd explored the area for the cave but was unable to find it. He walked the narrow canyons and ridges nearby, which supported slices of mountain habitat, and discovered edible flora, including the nuts from piñon pines. He couldn't recall from his research last year what the names of the rock monuments were except for the Siamese Twins and Balanced Rock. He made up his own names. There was Whitey, Saddleback, Kissing Turtles, Titanic, Momma with Kids, and the Church. They were now his winter family. They would be his guiding light, his beacon during the coming winter.

On the east side of the Garden, he found a strip of cottonwoods following the course of a possible seasonal stream or springs just below the surface. The land was thick with soil, quite the opposite from the rest of the area. It could've been a great farm, a homestead, somewhere to raise a family.

Not too far above the Farm, as he named it, Red found a series of concave depressions in the side of a ridge. Had they been deeper and had a smaller opening, they would've provided good shelter during the winter. He searched over the next several days for the large Cave of the Winds. He crossed over the area three or four times.

All of his calculations had gotten him this far. So, why was he now unable to find the renowned cave? Even a boy should have been able to find it. *That's it! A boy!* The Cave of the Winds had a man-made entrance. A small hole had originally been found by two boys playing in the mountains. The area had then been excavated, revealing a massive underground cave. "You stupid idiot!" How could he have forgotten? He was in a land without people. Why would the opening be there now?

He'd come so far. Winter was imminent. He would die without the cave.

A light snow came each day, and with it brought an increasing fear that he wouldn't be able to locate winter shelter. Red went back to the area of the shallow grottos on the ridge across from the Farm and scouted it again. He found a deeper depression on the leeward side of the ridge. It measured about seven feet high, thirteen feet wide, and four feet deep. It was completely open in front and would only protect him on one side. It wasn't good. But there were no better options.

The Farm had plenty of trees so Red could harvest aspen and cottonwood and make lodge poles to cover the front of his cave. He couldn't have a fire inside of the cave because of the smoke, but the ground in front provided him with a front-porch prow. He would've felt more secure if the cave were higher on the cliff, but being at ground level would have its own benefits. He'd no longer call it a cave. It was his fort.

Each day, Red would travel down to the Farm and harvest straight young aspen trees. After de-limbing them, he'd drag them two at a time back to the fort. He made a wall and covered the opening. Big rocks were levered to the outside and set at the base of three-quarters of the lodge poles. He left an open area wide enough for his passage. His supply of paracord secured the lodge poles together, top and bottom, in an upright position.

He used the discarded pile of branches and leaves to form a mattress inside the fort. He covered the mattress with one of his small tarps and placed his sleeping bag on top of it. It was the best accommodations he'd had in months. *Four and a half stars, I'd say.* He opened the small ziplock baggie that contained Addy's perfumed hanky. He closed his eyes and breathed in the sweet aroma he had been so familiar with over the years. Addy was standing in front of him, he was sure. He carefully resealed the baggie and placed it onto his bed.

He patted the mattress and lay down for a trial run. Red closed his eyes and remembered a man's voice. It was his acquaintance, Ed Morrison: "If you think I'm gonna sleep on the ground, you're crazy."

They'd been doing business together for over a year. Morrison usually walked into the office unannounced and gave no thought to the arrogant interruption. It was Morrison who'd encouraged Red to obtain his real estate license. Morrison was married and spoke very

AUTHOR'S NOTE

Behind the story *Behind Picketwire*.

It was an accidental meeting in a parking lot in my small town of Paradise, California. The old man's white hair, thick and spiky, matched his neatly trimmed goatee. It caught my attention. No, maybe it was his bright-blue eyes and that little-boy smile. His gait was strong and sure. He smiled at me, a total stranger. In that moment, Howard Johnson became my friend. That's what he was to most everyone. Our religious beliefs, contradictory lifestyles, childhood disparities, and the generation between us made not a difference in our friendship.

He was a Christian, a husband to Maurine, a father to a blended family, a businessman, real estate broker, a mayor, but most seriously, an impassioned hunter. "I wrote a book," he once said to me. "It's about my life, my hunting." It was a self-published paperback documenting a lifetime of his hunting excursions. Generations of local historical knowledge and lore took the reader on a solitary journey throughout Northern California.

Howard loved the Sacramento Valley and dreamt of seeing it in its natural state, prior to civilization. Flora, fauna, and wildlife; topography, astronomy, and meteorology; trials, tribulations, and survival; and his passions, wishes, and regrets were voiced within the 252 pages of a book called *Picketwire* (2008). There was no ending, no mention of what "Picketwire" signified, just stories of his hunting adventures, a journal of sorts. He figured if someone really wanted to know what he meant by the title, they would find out for themselves. And that was Howard.

Howard and I shared a love of stories and the yearning to pass them on. The concept was strong, and a story was there, hiding behind the name "Picketwire." He wanted the story told to the world and asked me to write it. The next several years of my rewrites were filled with research on topics to which I had limited exposure. I traveled the country, in the footsteps of my protagonist Red, ending in southern Colorado at the end of the Picketwire River.

Before my story was completed, Howard passed away from Alzheimer's disease in June 2014. One of the last fluid conversations I had with Howard was regarding how much he loved his wife and how he regretted never quite telling her enough. "With her is the only place I want to be." Howard considered himself a simple man. He worked hard, loved his family, and did business with a handshake. *Behind Picketwire* is a story about how significant and precious a seemingly ordinary life can be.

When I wrote about Red, my heart saw Howard. The character Addy is modeled after his beautiful wife, Maurine, always full of grace and strength. Matthew, after Howard's son, Michael, a man with nothing but love and respect for his father. And Jake, after my big red dog named Blue. Howard was buried in the Old Magalia cemetery, in Magalia, California, just a little above Paradise, where towering Sawmill Peak stands sentry over him.

I finished our book, Howard.

M. Day Hampton, 2020

ABOUT THE AUTHOR

M. Day Hampton currently lives in Paradise, California. After hearing a survivalist anecdote from a dear friend, Hampton was inspired to complete the journey described in this book through the American wilderness. *Behind Picketwire* is Hampton's debut novel.

Made in USA - Kendallville, IN
1183002_9781734696608
10.20.2020 0931